Legacy of Love

Author's Revised Edition

by
Marianne K. Martin

Bella
BOOKS

Ferndale, Michigan
2003

Bella Books, Inc.
P.O. Box 201007
Ferndale, MI 48220

First published 1997 by Naiad Press
Printed in the United States of America on acid-free paper
First Edition

Cover designer: Bonnie Liss (Phoenix Graphics)

ISBN 1-931513-15-5

For Jo
Who knew from the beginning

Acknowledgments

This is a thank you, long overdue, to two wonderful women who at different times were such an important part of my formal education. Harriet Pitts long ago nurtured the shy beginnings of expression, and continually told me that I must write. And, Barbara Fausell, through her literary foresight and quiet example, gave me the courage to write from my soul. It just took me a very long time.

And, so that these do not become overdue, I offer my thanks and immeasurable gratitude to:

Rebecca, friend and "agent", whose drive and commitment is invaluable.

Friend and "support system" Teressa, from whom I have gathered so many needed positives and tucked them safely away.

Barbara Grier and Donna McBride for bravely blazing such a wide, wonderful trail of opportunity.

Bonnie Liss and Phoenix Graphics for presenting my first "baby" to the world so beautifully.

Love and gratitude that will take a lifetime to express to my best friend and partner, Jo, who never allows me to settle for less than my best and whose loyal and unconditional love is the most important thing in my life.

INTRODUCTION

In 1997, Barbara Grier at Naiad Press took a chance on this new writer and published *Legacy of Love* as my first novel. I will always be grateful to her for that chance. Subsequently, Naiad Press published my next three novels.

Now, as Barbara Grier and Donna McBride gradually take Naiad Press into retirement, Bella Books has graciously picked up the publishing rights to *Legacy*. I am equally thrilled to have my first "baby" reborn under this new press.

Bella owners Kelly Smith and Terese Orban have asked me to re-insert the chapters cut from the original printing, and I am more than pleased to oblige. These newly included chapters add important insights into the character of Sage Bristo, so now as you read this version it is hoped that you will enjoy Sage as she was meant to be seen.

Part I

Part I

Chapter 1

How merely the sound of the voice on the answering machine still could make her heart jump so was beyond logic. Sage Bristo smiled as she listened to its message. "Love, I'm staying in town this weekend. Meet me at the apartment tonight. Brad's flight isn't due until 9:20 Sunday evening."

Her smile remained as she quickly stripped and headed for the shower. Spending the weekend in the city meant two things. They would *not* be riding at the house in Kingston, sharing the time with Suzanne's six-year-old daughter and four-year-old-son. They would instead be spending time meeting more intimate needs, ones pressing to be fulfilled.

Weekends like these, many over the past two years, allowed her to entertain the dream of a committed relationship with Suzanne Weber. In that dream Suzanne leaves her husband of eight years, moves with her to another part of the country, and raises her children with her. A pipe dream, NaNan would have called it, the kind that rose in the smoke of the old one's pipes and dissipated quickly into transparent air. Maybe so, she thought, maybe so.

She donned a gray silk blouse, leaving the top two buttons unfastened. Soft wool charcoal pants neatly hugged her trim waist. Sage gazed thoughtfully into the mist of the partially steamed mirror. What did women like about her? What made someone like Suzanne chance so much to be with her? She wondered if whatever it was would always be there.

With eyes of darkest brown splashed with flecks of brightness, she watched her long slender hand carefully guide the brush through the short gentle curls. Every fourth week, like clockwork, the natural brown curls were meticulously snipped just past half a turn and shaped over her ears. Dark lashes and brows scoffed at makeup and drew envy from women she dated. Sage dipped her finger into the Vaseline and smoothed it neatly over her lips. Low maintenance, she mused, remembering Suzanne's pain at having eyeliner permanently tattooed.

Maybe her looks alone attracted women to her. Androgynous to be sure. Pure and natural. A perfect 5 on the Loulan scale. Perhaps they liked her manner of confidence, movements and thought always sure and decisive. Or, was she only a mystery to them, a challenge to unravel? Knowing was probably useless anyway; she was who she was. She didn't see that changing much. Finding out what made the difference between sex and love, between pleasure and happiness, was of much greater importance. The years had provided ample opportunity to explore sexual pleasure, but she'd experienced very little love and happiness in her life. Sage Bristo dared hope for them only cautiously.

With maturity came more positive thoughts of the future, leaving little room for those wasted on the past. Useless they

4

were, except for the memories of Cimmie and NaNan; the rarities of her past worthy of remembrance. They formed the oasis of her life, where she had been healed and loved. The only place in her young life where who she was, was treasured, and the uniqueness of her spirit celebrated; in the heart of her sister, in the arms of her grandmother.

In those arms she had heard the stories from early childhood. She had listened intently to them, the "ramblings of an old woman" as her mother put it, and believed. *Sage*, NaNan called her, not *Celia*. "It's more becoming to your spirit," she told her. "The blooms in my garden droop without water, break in hard winds. But you, like sage, find nutrients where you can, and grow strong through it all. Your beauty blooms in my heart. You bring me back to a heritage I lost so long ago. The one that connects my soul with the earth and its waters, to the sun and the wind. Here in my garden I search for strength for my spirit to stay connected with the women who worked the soil and governed the longhouses. But, there it is, in you. You have a strong Seneca spirit," she said, straightening her frail bones. "*Orenda* marks your soul. You walk tall, with the pride of a warrior, yet butterflies rest on your hands."

Sage's throat began to tighten. She closed her eyes for a second and swallowed hard. Memories were important. She would always allow time for them, always be careful to keep them clear and true. And someday she would find a way to pass them on. But never again would she be able to ask the questions that troubled her soul; never again would she feel the gentle hand in hers. Only in her mind could she see her grandmother's twinkling eyes and hear the pride in her voice as she spoke of spirits and clans and a heritage more valued than wealth. She missed her. Desperately.

5

Chapter 2

The distance between her Village flat and Suzanne's East Side apartment was not great. However, there was no such thing as a quick jaunt through Manhattan on a Friday night. Sage worked her way through the congestion without complaint, because for now she had to. A lifetime of exposure to the city had resulted in remarkable maneuverability skills, but, it would take more than that for her to live here forever. The time would come when she would leave the city that never sleeps and find a place where the only light of the night was that of the moon. She longed for a quieter place, where the sounds of the night whisper on the wind, where her soul could stretch and her mind relax. Sage Bristo needed to drive fast on long stretches of country road, to feel a powerful horse under her commanding rein, to find unconditional love in the embrace of a beautiful woman. And she would. Someday.

The wealthy Manhattan neighborhood, with its massive apartment houses and mansions overlooking Central Park, could easily be intimidating. But Sage Bristo was familiar with wealth. She had been born of it and disowned by it. The possession of wealth for her, was at the same time desirable and loathsome. She struggled with believing in its omnipotence, but not in its influence.

She slipped security his customary bill. He was well paid for his discretionary silence. The elevator took her swiftly to the top floor and the Weber apartment. As she had done so many times before, she let herself in.

"In here, Love," Suzanne called from the living room. She sat in the middle of the green leather sofa, shoulder-length blond hair tucked behind one ear and falling gently forward from the other. Her beauty was universal; lithe and fair. She was a vision in misty green and white, sorting through bills and messages.

"The kids with your mom?"

"Uh, huh. She's been looking forward to this weekend with them."

"So have I." Sage's seductive stare met Suzanne's pretty smile.

"Why don't you fix us a drink while I finish up the mail. Then I'm all yours." She winked at the smile on Sage's face.

Placing the drink on the glass table, Sage settled comfortably close to her lover.

"Goddamn him!" Suzanne blurted the words, as she threw a reservation confirmation on the table. "He's going to spend the weekend he'd promised to the kids golfing in Connecticut. He never spends time with them."

The only time Sage ever heard Suzanne swear was in reaction to Brad. And the increased frequency had become no-

7

ticeable. "Suzanne, he's making you more and more frustrated and angry. It's not healthy. Maybe it's time to leave him."

"Don't start, Sage." After a deep breath, her tone softened. "Please, honey. You know it's not possible."

"No, I don't know that." Sage cupped Suzanne's pretty face in her hand. "Look, the kids like me, don't they?"

"They adore you, as I do."

"I make decent money. Not as much as I'd like, but I can take care of you and the kids. We could be a real family."

"As little attention as he gives those kids, you'd think it would be that easy. As I've told you before, I know Brad would never let me have the kids, especially if he knew I was with a woman."

"We'll fight for them. Other lesbians have won custody."

"It would take every cent we have. And it would mean sacrificing life as I know it. Brad would exhaust all our resources. What kind of future would that leave the kids? We've discussed this before Sage. I'm not willing to go through that."

The words held no revelation. Sage hadn't been so naive as to think a relationship with Suzanne Weber would be an easy one. Yet the love she felt for her wouldn't let her give it up, regardless of how difficult it became. She pulled Suzanne into her arms and kissed her, melting into her softness, fighting a nagging uneasiness that had bothered her all month.

Sage's slender fingers lifted and stroked Suzanne's silky golden hair. "What do you want from me?" Sage whispered the words softly against her ear.

"I need you to love me . . . as long as you possibly can."

Sage closed her eyes and nodded gently against her head.

The night held their passion, clothed their secret in darkness, and muffled their cries of desire as they reached for

8

ecstasy over and over again. They shut out the world, narrowed it to what they could see and touch, narrowed it to each other. For now it would be enough.

Morning sunlight streamed through the large bedroom window, washing its warmth over the partially covered women. They slept very little; not wanting to waste precious time. Sage stirred; her morning eyes opened to the soft repose of her lover's body. Crisp green sheets intersected the gentle feminine curves. Golden strands of hair tumbled across the pillow, shining in the brightness.

Sage slipped quietly from the bed and returned minutes later with a glass of orange juice for them to share. Sitting on the edge of the bed, dressed only in the open-front silk blouse, she tenderly brushed the hair from Suzanne's face and kissed her awake.

"Mmm, I thought I was having a wonderful dream," Suzanne said in a quiet, sleepy voice. "But you're really here."

"With nourishment," she smiled, handing her the glass.

"You are wonderful." They traded sips until the juice was gone, then Suzanne reached under the silk, and brought Sage down to her.

Sage's flesh, cooled by the morning air, warmed quickly against Suzanne's skin. With renewed energy, their passion ignited once again. Suzanne pressed into Sage's embrace, her body making demands of her skillful hands, commanding pleasure from her exciting mouth. Sage gave willingly, unselfishly. Her single intent, her only mission, was fulfilling her lover. Suzanne's gratification was paramount. Every touch from Sage's hand brought her lover closer. Every whisper from her lips increased the sweetness of her flow. Appreciation shone on the now glistening skin and sounded in the love-labored breathing.

Suzanne gave herself to Sage, wholly and completely. She took her lips hungrily. Every part of her mind and body belonged to Sage. There was no other moment except this one, no other desire but to be filled with this woman's love. "You make me want nothing but you," Suzanne gasped with shortened breath.

Her whisper was hot against Suzanne's breast. "I'll give you as much love as you want."

Matching her lover's rhythm, Sage moved with exquisite intent, feeling the pleasure she was giving deep within herself. She felt the power of her sensuality welling inside Suzanne, pushing her hips powerfully against her thigh. The burst of heat traveled, powerfully melting its way, centering itself at her very soul. Hot flesh touched upon hot flesh. She gave of her heat, her passion, to every part of Suzanne. Her mouth was ardent and eager, fiercely exciting Suzanne everywhere she touched. One place treated no less than another. Pleasing Suzanne was innate for Sage; the effects registered through her senses. Suzanne's moans turned to urgent gasps of air. Her sounds spurned Sage on, sending her arousal to new heights. She tasted the salty flow, embraced the undulating hips with her hands. Pleasure had become necessity now. Sage felt Suzanne's swelling urgency, heard her cries. And at the very height of passion, heard her name screamed over and over. From within Sage felt the powerful, unmistakable spasm of orgasm.

Suzanne gasped forth the words, "Oh, god . . . oh, god, Sage . . . don't stop, honey . . . please don't stop yet." Gloriously tender fingers caressed her from within, until they brought complete and utter satisfaction.

Sage nestled her chest into the silken heat, wrapped her arms around the expressive hips, and pressed her face against the shuddering plane of Suzanne's abdomen.

"Goddamn. You are good," came a male voice from the doorway of the children's room.

The startled women looked quickly; snatched abruptly from their intimacy. Brad Weber stood open-shirted in the doorway, his hand in his unzipped pants. "Am I to thank you for not desecrating *my* bed?"

Suzanne turned her head away in shock and embarrassment. Sage quickly removed herself from between Suzanne's legs, and covered her with the sheet.

"So I was right," he continued, to Sage's unabashed eye contact. "My darling wife, you look so surprised." He laughed, his hand moving rhythmically in his pants. "Don't worry, this doesn't have to be a problem." His eyes followed Sage as she buttoned her blouse. "All you have to do is take care of me that well." He began to close the distance to the bed.

Suzanne sat up abruptly, clutching the sheet over her breasts. "Stop it, Brad," she shouted. "At least allow her to dress in private."

"I think your friend and I should get better acquainted first. You won't have to work nearly as hard to make me happy." His eyes roamed the tall figure standing defiantly at the end of the bed.

Sage was direct, unrattled. "You don't get it do you?"

"Don't, Sage," Suzanne pleaded. "Just leave. This isn't going to get any better." She grabbed a robe from the bottom of the bed and slipped it on.

Sage turned her attention directly to Suzanne. "Come with me, Suzanne. We're right down to it, honey. If you're going to do it, you have to do it now."

"No, you're the one who doesn't get it," interrupted Brad. "She'll never throw away everything for someone like you, no matter how well you make her climb the walls."

Pulling her clothes on, Sage tried again. "Come with me," she said, watching what she knew were farewell tears making their way down Suzanne's beautiful cheeks.

"You know why," Suzanne managed through increasing emotion. "You know how I feel about you."

"You will always need the arms of a woman. You'll long for the love of a woman until you die. But it won't be me, not unless you leave with me now." Sage picked up her jacket from the chair, and stopped. Suzanne was sobbing, her face buried in her knees.

With a deep breath, Sage raised her head tall. She left briskly, brushing hard against Brad's shoulder as she passed, his warning ringing in her ears.

"If there ever is another woman, she dammed well better be bi."

Radio blaring, Sage made her way aggressively down Westside, toward the interstate. Her mind was reeling. She struggled against her emotions. The improbability had been there from the start. Hadn't she felt it all along? The suddenness was difficult to be sure, but tears were no good now. They were only useless emotion. She wouldn't do it. She wouldn't cry.

She would drive fast, speeding mile after mile, road after road, testing the edge of control. And she would drink, one glass after another, day after day; blurring the edges, until one day blended into another. But she would not cry.

Chapter 3

This is my day — empty hours waiting for me to fill them however I choose. The reminder was still in place in Sage's mind, as it had been since she was a child. It had begun as a morning ritual, NaNan waking her for school, declaring the day fresh and new, and Sage joining her to claim the day. Its purpose was obvious even then — no matter how bad yesterday had been, she had the opportunity to make today better. A lesson NaNan had made sure that she learned early. Over the years the lesson had proven it's worth; beatings and dark closets, disappointments and love affairs gone bad could not be changed, only left behind.

Today is no different. Suzanne, and all feelings good or

bad associated with her, must be left behind. This is my day — empty hours waiting for me to fill them however I choose.

Westbrooke's Assistant Director slipped quickly through the doorway of Sage's office. "Will you take line one, please? Ella King's daughter, and she'll speak to no one except the Director."

"I've got it," she said with a wave. "Check on the meat delivery."

She picked up the phone and relaxed against the back of her chair. "Westbrooke Senior Living. This is Sage Bristo, how can I help you?" Sage listened with only passing interest as the woman on the other end of the phone voiced her complaint. "Was your mother's name marked clearly on the label? . . . It's not unusual for something to come back from the laundry in the wrong basket . . . I understand. I'll look for the dress personally . . . That's no problem, she'll have her dress by tomorrow . . . You're welcome."

She added the search to the already long list for the day and made a mental note. New or not, the dress wasn't likely to be something the twenty-something staff would steal. She'd make room-by-room visits tonight until she found it. Westbrooke residents had enough to deal with without losing what few personal effects they could still call their own. *At least this one visits enough to know when her mother is missing something.*

Movement at her office door caught Sage's attention before she could decide which task on her list could get her out from behind her desk. Molly Berger's head of thin gray hair peeked around the doorjamb.

Sage motioned her in and watched the stooped figure, aided by a cane, make her way through the doorway. "How are you today, Molly?"

The old woman stopped and hunched further forward, both hands on the top of her cane. "I'm no older than tomorrow," she said, looking up to make eye contact. "But I'm no younger than today."

The response she had expected. Sage smiled. Westbrooke's little philosopher had a stranger than usual resemblance to Yoda today.

"Then I'll assume that today is the best we can hope for."

"I suppose it is," she nodded.

"So what can I do for you, Molly, to make today the best it can be?"

With a little grin Molly tilted her head. "Come and talk," she said. "I'll fix us tea with a little edge."

"A treat I can appreciate," Sage said with a wink, "and a secret I can keep."

"Wouldn't have asked you otherwise."

"Let me make a couple of calls and I'll be right there."

To many, the therapeutic benefits of a spot of special tea and a talk with a ninety-one year old woman would go unrecognized. But for as long as Sage could remember it was an old woman's wisdom that had taught her what was good and right, that showed her the worth of life and a world she would otherwise have never known. She knew that slowness of gait didn't indicate slowness of mind, and pauses in conversation weren't lapses in memory as much as time needed to search through years of experiences and thoughts. Patience, she found, could reap pearls of knowledge that it would take her own mind years to cultivate.

Among the pearls she had gleaned from NaNan was that focusing on someone else's needs, Cimmie's, Suzanne's, her residents, helped to ease the pain of her own needs going unmet. Today, her focus would be on Molly Berger, and she would get through. Tomorrow was tomorrow.

Molly sipped her tea, surrounded by the few personal belongings that the tiny room would accommodate. There were pictures everywhere, some on the limited wall space, most in dozens of different frames sitting in staggered rows on every table surface. Pictures of a husband in younger years, children in graduation gowns and wedding dresses, and grandchildren and more grandchildren. Memories of a life nearing its realization. Proof of its fulfillment and of its worth.

Sage picked up the little silver frame near the front of the table. "So this is the newest grandbaby," she said with a closer look.

Molly nodded. "Lee Tyler is great-great-grandbaby number five. He's already walking since I last held him." She reached a slightly shaky hand out to receive the picture from Sage. "I'm missing so much of their lives," she said, touching the picture with her fingertips. "They don't trust an old woman to baby sit anymore. Oh, that's not what they say, but I know what they mean." She handed the picture back to Sage. "Other times I know they're too busy."

Sage returned the picture to its position of honor. "We get caught up in day to day living and forget how important things are to us."

"Why is it that *you* make time for an old woman when you don't have to?"

"Because I didn't always," Sage returned, as the pale blue eyes studied her. "And it was the most painful lesson I've ever learned."

"But, you see, the value of the lesson has added that measure to your life. That's how the pain is stopped. It's the lessons that go unlearned that continue the ripples of pain out into the world."

Sage smiled. "Now you know why I sip tea with you, Molly. You have a way of turning my pain into something acceptable. My grandmother was the only other person I knew who could do that."

Molly sipped of her tea, relishing the taste with a purse of her lips. "So you have pain, too." She nodded as she spoke. "We help each other I think. That's what gets me by these days. Not much here to keep an old woman busy."

"Wasting time and thought on things you can do nothing about only causes frustration and anger — negative energy — You find yourself searching for irrational solutions. Keeping busy has kept me out of therapy, I'm sure."

Molly nodded and lifted her cup.

She wasn't going to say it today and Sage wasn't going to ask. But she knew. All Molly Berger wanted was to go home. To be in the house where she had lived for sixty-five years, to tend her garden, and hand feed the squirrel that she had coaxed to her windowsill. She no doubt still wonders how long her little friend came looking for her before it gave up.

The one thing that Sage knew would make Molly happy, she couldn't do for her. Not even for a day, and not because company policy wouldn't allow it. She couldn't take Molly home for good, and a visit would be too disheartening. Seeing the changes that strangers had made to her home, or worse, maybe seeing it neglected and in disrepair. Surely it would be better to leave untouched the memories of her life there. Memories of joy, giving birth to her children in her own bedroom — sad memories of her father's death in his favorite chair. Wouldn't it be best not to chance the disrespect of strangers who couldn't know anything of the life that had been lived there?

Her thoughts were interrupted by Molly's offer to refill her cup. Sage declined, and asked with a tilt of her head, "Do you think you could come up with a convincing reason to be near the delivery entrance in about thirty minutes? In case anyone asks?"

Molly's eyes brightened with excitement. "Sometimes being an old woman has its advantages," she said with a smile. "Most of the time they think we're wandering without purpose. No one bothers to ask — except you."

Sage rose with a mental shake of her head. That was the attitude that went straight to the heart of how her residents were treated. "Traveling clothes," Sage said with a wink, "half an hour."

Chapter 4

"Where are we going?" Molly asked, settled comfortably in the front seat of Sage's car.

"A special place I visit once a week. I thought it would be nice to have good company today."

"It must be special enough to risk being fired."

Sage gave Molly her best smile. "The company is."

The hour and a half drive through traffic and lights was barely noticed. They talked of politics now and politics then. Of Molly's work in the factory and losing her husband to the war. And of losing the job that supported four children when the war ended. They talked of freedom and the power of the vote and how the world was still changing.

For Sage it was a lesson in perspective. Balance to an

ancient history, learned of through her grandmother, of a powerful nation ruled by women, and its destruction by the Europeans. A reminder of how much the struggle has been able to regain, and a tiny glimmer of hope that someday the struggle could bring society full circle.

The two-story brick house stood unpretentiously on the edge of a middle-class neighborhood. Boxwoods and low-growing junipers softened the lines of a thick-pillared porch that covered the width of the house. Its age was evident more by style than by condition, and by the maturity of the maples lining the street. The doctor had lived fugally and invested wisely. If he had not seen the need to spend it on a lavish lifestyle while he was alive, NaNan had seen no need to spend it on such after her husband was gone. Their philosophy that one person's excess should fill another's need had joined them together in life, and now could be carried on beyond their deaths.

"Your grandmother's house," Molly said as the car came to a stop in the drive. "What a nice old place."

"It's nothing fancy, but it's always been beautiful to me." As she got out of the car her eyes lingered over the side of the house — curtains draped partially across the upstairs windows, the vines of ivy clinging tightly to the brick of the porch and creeping silently along the wall from window to window.

Sage breathed deeply. If only she could open the back door and smell the bread baking in the old iron oven, and walk up behind her grandmother and wrap her arms around the tiny frame and hug her for a long minute. If only once more she could smell the scent of Windsong on NaNan's old cardigan sweater and feel the safety of her arms. If only she could just go home.

She offered Molly her arm in lieu of a cane. "Come around back, there's something I want you to see."

They made slow, steady progress toward an old arch-top wooden gate at the rear of the house. There was no fence, only the gentle droop of mature forsythia bordering the length of the lot. And the yard, all fifty by seventy-five feet of it, was a garden in full spring bloom.

"Oh my," Molly whispered as they passed through the gate. "Oh my, oh my."

Sage smiled. "I thought you'd like this. Are you up for a stroll down the middle? There's a bench there by the redbud."

But Molly was already in motion, nearly leaving Sage's arm in her haste. Their pace was perfect for appreciating the colors and textures, and the aromas that had so pleased NaNan. Sage pointed out her grandmother's favorite dianthus with its tiny pinked petals and explained where other plants would soon replace the spring blooms in the summer transformation.

The cycle of life in the garden, although learned and understood early in Sage's life, wasn't an easy lesson to apply. The process of life and death and rebirth was miraculous when it involved trillium and wisteria. But when it was family, when it was NaNan, or even Molly, it made her want to stop what could not be stopped. And the only thing that could ease the pain in her heart would be to experience the next phase of the cycle, to see the rebirth firsthand. Yet, as hard as she tried, Sage could not identify it in herself. It was an honor worthy of a better recipient.

Sage knelt beside the path and pulled new sprouts of clover and chickweed from between feathery leaves of silver mound.

"Do you feel her here?"

Sage nodded. "As if I could turn and touch her arm beside me."

"What is it that you miss most?"

"There is so much, it isn't possible to narrow it to one thing." She plucked young shoots of wild catnip and rubbed the minty leaf between her thumb and forefinger. "Her wisdom, her love — she raised me as her ancestors had raised their children. She loved unconditionally and taught through

21

example. There was no punishment except consequence. The longer it took me to do the chores the less time we had to go riding. When I broke a window we figured out together how I could earn the money to replace it."

Sage separated the leaves of catnip from the stem and placed them in Molly's hand.

"Mother Nature's air freshener," Molly said, rubbing them between her palms and bringing them to her nose.

"NaNan always left a section near the back steps for the catnip to grow. She picked fresh stems each week and kept them in the wastebasket and garbage can. I miss that smell."

"Do you think it's true that the heart grows fonder with absence?"

"It grows wiser for sure."

Molly nodded. "Without everyday distractions it's easier to see what's most important — what is real and true . . . We had a boy in our neighborhood who liked to set fires, set his house and garage on fire numerous times. Probably a half dozen times we found him in our basement when we returned home because my Ralph had forgotten to lock the side door. I was so mad at him. I used this accusatory tone that I knew got his attention and questioned how important the safety of his family was to him." Her eyes watered noticeably. "But you know, he never once forgot to tell me that he loved me before we went to sleep at night."

She placed her hand on Sage's. "You see, love is at the root of it. Love, passed from heart to heart, is the Legacy."

"I'm afraid that's the thing I'll never again have in my life, the kind of love that she gave me."

Molly reached over to tap her finger gently against Sage's chest. "It's right here," she said. "But to keep it you have to give it away."

But you can't give away what no one wants. Like avocado refrigerators and outdated clothing, love becomes clutter —

emotional clutter that takes up space better used for something else. It wasn't that she was questioning the old woman's wisdom, just its application. The rules of love just weren't the same.

Chapter 5

The hour was much too early, the sun much too bright. After a night at the club and only two hours of sleep, the last thing she would have planned was a 7:00 breakfast at The Bagel. Yet for as long as she could remember, nothing that Cimmie Capra asked was too much to accommodate. No one had ever adequately described the kind of love Sage felt for her sister; it transcended every definition she'd ever heard. They had developed a bond that was mutually protective, and enduring, and honest. It was deep and intense, without being sexual, caring without being judgmental, and fun without being superficial. Through twenty-six years it had grown and flourished, despite severe tests of abuse, separation, and prejudice. Push had often come to shove in the most literal sense, and they had always been there for each other.

"Hey, sunshine. Sit down and erase this sudden guilt I'm feeling. You look like 2:00 this afternoon would have been a better breakfast date." Cimmie smiled wide and comfortably, a stark contrast to Sage's reserved subtle smile, seen so infrequently. But the contrast only began there. The sisters presented opposite ends of the spectrum in many ways. Cimmie was softer and rounder, with long brown hair and a taste for bright colors; Sage, athletic and firm, had classic, conservative taste.

"I'll manage," Sage muttered, reaching for Cimmie's coffee.

"I don't know. It has to be serious when you resort to java."

"Life is a game masochists play." Sage gripped the cup with both hands. Heavy lids closed as she sipped the hot brew.

"Wanna tell me about it?"

"Mmm." It sounded somewhere between a loud sigh and a groan. "I'm an uncommitted woman again. Have been for a month now."

"So you're into self-inflicted pain therapy."

She forced a half laugh. "Yeah."

"Of all the women in the world you could have, and even the number I'm aware of astounds me, why her? Was she keeping you" — her tone turned sour — "like the soap opera queen?"

Sage set the cup down and hung her normally proud head. "For a while. Somewhere along the way, I lost control of things."

"Well, if by 'things', you mean your heart, that's something no one has control over. Love isn't something you easily fall out of."

Sage shook her head slowly. "Love is not something I plan on again. Anyway . . ." She straightened and looked with resolve into Cimmie's understanding eyes. "What's so early-morning important?"

"I'm sorry to have to add more bad news, but our father has called a family meeting for this afternoon. He wasn't specific, but I suspect he's soliciting support for another challenge of NaNan's will, her sanity I think."

The news wasn't a surprise. With inexhaustible resources, her father had been able to tie up the will in legal battles for four long years. Sage appreciated her sister's loyalty to her. She was now the only tie to a family she no longer belonged to, one she hadn't lived with since she was eleven, and one that had completely disowned her when she was fifteen. NaNan and Cimmie had been her family, even after the revelation of her lesbianism. She had even taken her grandmother's name. Yet he still couldn't leave it alone. For such wealth to be left to his disowned daughter was more than John Jeremy Capra could take. He would not allow it.

"I'll call my attorney and see if she's heard anything yet. Thanks for warning me."

"I'm sorry, Sage. I've tried, but there's no reasoning with him."

"Cim, don't you dare put yourself in jeopardy." The tone of her voice was firm and insistent. "You know how I feel about your challenging him."

"Too many years spent fearing and avoiding his wrath is starting to make me hate myself. You've always faced it for both of us whenever you could. Even as a child, I felt guilt for allowing you to do that. I love you too much to look the other way. It's about time I grew up."

"You have nothing to feel guilty about. I chose to defy him. You were always there when I needed you. Don't do anything stupid. Promise me." Sage reached across the table and took Cimmie's hand. The emotion in her eyes surpassed parental concern. "Let my attorney do it."

"I promise," she relented. "It's no wonder women lose their senses around you," she mused, watching the corners of her sister's mouth curl slightly upward. "You don't even have to try, do you?"

"Well, what I get and what I need, haven't met as yet." Sage squeezed and released her sister's hand. "So, I'll go to the parties, and go to the club with Pat and let her think that it's her mission to introduce me to the one woman who can make me forget all others." *No one gets the power to make my life miserable, not John Capra, not then and not now. And certainly not Suzanne. I may not be able to stop the negatives, but how I react to them is my choice.*

Cimmie searched Sage's pretty brown eyes, so like her own. "Someday, you're going to let someone in there" — she pointed at Sage's chest — "who's going to see you with her heart, not just her eyes. Meantime, I guess I'm the one who has to make sure you have breakfast."

Chapter 6

"How long are you going to tease the poor woman?" Pat was shouting across the table, trying to be heard over the club's music.

Sage returned an I-don't-know-what-you're-talking-about-look and sipped her drink. She liked Pat, the only person besides her sister who dared tease her so relentlessly. She was refreshingly irreverent.

"She sends over a drink, and you get up and dance with someone else? You're arrogant Sage, downright arrogant."

Sage leaned forward over her drink. "She's dangerous."

"She's gorgeous," Pat countered.

"She's straight."

Pat screwed her thin features into an expression of cynicism. "That's never stopped you before." The music softened momentarily. "What? Have you lost your sense of adventure?" Another friend left the table, and Pat slid into the seat next to Sage.

Sage's lips curled into a slight grin. "Go give her a thrill, my friend. She's all yours."

"Yeah, like she's interested in this bag of bones. I've got to stop going out with you; the comparison is killing me. Believe me, if I had your appeal, I'd bed down every beautiful woman that dared get within arm's distance."

"I swear, Pat, you should've been a man."

Pat laughed her always raspy, often impudent laugh. "What is it they say? I'm just a man trapped in this hideously feminine body." She placed her long bony fingers as femininely as she could over the flatness of her chest and burst into laughter again.

As they laughed comfortably together, two women made their way between the tightly placed seats to approach their table.

"Would you mind if we joined you for a drink?" The voice was silky smooth, carried on Chloe-scented air.

Sage's gaze followed the sexy lines, outlined in tight blue, up to the dark eyes and dark hair of the woman who had watched her all evening. Pat had already invited her and her fair redheaded friend to have a seat. Introductions were made all around, and fresh drinks mingled with small talk, while the woman named Lisa made her intent clear. Her eyes, filled with inquiry, took in every expression, watched every move Sage made. As they spoke, she moved closer, allowing her arm to brush Sage's, and her thigh to make contact under the table.

"How about a dance, ladies. If I don't start moving around, I'm going to be too drunk to find my way home." Pat's invitation seemed to be exactly what the women wanted. They accepted readily.

Dance after dance, Lisa's feminine form gradually pressed tighter into Sage's embrace. The ritual was a familiar one; Sage's strong, classically trained lead, allowed the decision for closeness to be made by her partner. The inevitable positive decision attested to Sage's sexual appeal, and proved to be a tremendous turn-on.

Lisa's body, full of breast and narrow of waist, moved rhythmically against Sage's trim, tight form. "You're a wonderful dancer." Both arms slid suggestively around Sage's shoulders, and Lisa whispered against the softness of her neck. "You lead better —" She caught herself, burying the last words.

"Better than a man?" Sage asked against the dark curls. "You didn't think it was a secret that you're straight, did you?"

"I'm not so sure that's true." Lisa was speaking close to Sage's face, avoiding eye contact. The music took a livelier turn. "Is there somewhere we could talk?"

Sage took her hand and led her through the moving mass to a secluded hallway behind the bathroom. She had talked with other women there. How many, she couldn't remember. It was there Suzanne had cried in her arms, confessing her attraction to her. A flood of emotion suddenly ravaged her cloak of austerity; trying to tear down her only protection. She didn't want to know what she was feeling; love, sadness, anger. What difference did it make? She pulled the cloak tighter. Lisa's arms slid around her waist. Chloe scented-hair brushed across Sage's face. Sexual excitement sneaked quietly under the cloak, as Lisa's warmth pressed against her. Instinct nullified the thought that she should walk, right now. She began doing things she knew would make Lisa's body disregard all the rules. Her hands moved intuitively, drifted confidently, challenged the boundaries.

Soft skin smelling of makeup brushed delicately over Sage's face and neck. The invitation was obvious. Sage slid her hand tenderly under the curls covering Lisa's neck and ear. Dark blue eyes opened into Sage's. "You're a beautiful woman, Lisa."

"Then kiss me," she breathed softly.

Sage lowered her eyes, touching their lips together with deliberate tenderness. Lisa's initial tentativeness easily yielded into full warm contact. The soft intermittent touches of their lips soon blended into a series of sensual kisses. Lips parted; warm wetness invited temptation. They explored and tasted. Lisa's fingers laced into Sage's hair, pulled her in deeper. Arousal stirred deeply, distinctively. Lisa's breathing quickened. Mutual desire manifested itself in a low moan, as Sage left her mouth and quickly found the tender skin below Lisa's ear.

"I didn't know if I could feel like this for a woman." Lisa's words, carried on warm air, breathed past Sage's ear.

How many times had Sage heard their message, responded to their excitement. Their delivery varied; sometimes they were said in a whisper, sometimes in resonant ecstasy. But the meaning was always the same: "I've always wondered." And then, she reminded herself, when they're through wondering . . . they remember the rules. Suzanne's face was so annoyingly clear in Sage's mind. Her eyes, burning with uncertainty, still haunted her unmercifully. Lisa's lips were enticing, but they might as well have been Suzanne's.

Lisa's hips pressed their heat into her now, sending their message loud and clear. The words steamed against her mouth. "Is this where you invite me to your place?"

Sage looked into Lisa's eyes, Suzanne's eyes. "No," she said, separating them more gently than her words. "This is where I leave you to your fantasy."

* * * * *

31

Leaving the smoky atmosphere of the bar alone, she breathed in the tainted night air and headed for the car. The decision felt right; the control felt good again. It would be this way now, on her terms. Emotion was back where it belonged; temptation was overcome. Maybe she would sleep well tonight.

Then, in the space of a blink, too sudden for fear to even register, a man blocked the path to her car. He laughed menacingly, as a large rough hand covered her mouth from behind. She prayed it was the car they wanted. But when her keys struck the concrete and the man's eyes remained fixed, she knew it was not. An icy grip of fear claimed her as tightly as the viselike grip on her body. Her mind screamed out for help; silent screams in vain. She struggled against panic and its resulting weakness. She fought for control over it, for the strength to fight the best fight she could. Instinct, honed by years of practice, took over. She would not let them see fear in her, would not allow them any more power. With a powerful kick, she landed a blow between the legs of the approaching man. He doubled in pain. "You fuckin' cunt licker," he growled. "Do her, Bobby."

The man named Bobby immediately lifted her body, threw her to the ground, and dropped the full weight of his body on top of her. The impact knocked the air from her lungs with a cough. Dazed from her head hitting the concrete, Sage opened her eyes to the barrel of a gun pointed at her face by the man she had just kicked in the groin. Death was suddenly a personal reality. *This is where it will happen, here in the filth, at the hands of hatred.* The tremendous weight of the man on top of her shifted, shooting sharp pain through her right leg. He was unfastening his pants, cursing at the difficulty of doing so while keeping her mouth covered. She looked again at the man standing above her nervously holding the gun. Hope for life fleeted, leaving her with one solitary thought. *Let me die before they do this.* She fought with every ounce of strength she had.

Her strength, and apparent lack of fear, surprised both men. She heard the sound of the gun being readied. The weight again collapsed on her, pushing the air painfully from her lungs. "Goddamn it! Don't shoot her! Get down here. I want her to feel this." The man shoved the gun into the waist of his jeans, and quickly came to Bobby's aid. He crushed Sage's left arm beneath the weight of his knee, while he leaned across her to cover her mouth with one hand, and pin her right arm to the ground with the other. The large meaty hand partially blocked her nose. Instinctively, Sage struggled to breathe. The putrid smell of body odor and maleness was the only air available.

Suddenly the weight shifted again, and her shirt was ripped open. For a brief moment her hips were free. She used them to fight hard against the rough hands trying to rip open her jeans. The weight returned. "You're hell-bent on dyin' ain't you, dyke? Well it ain't gonna be that easy." He held the shiny blade of a hunting knife in her line of sight before touching the razor-sharp edge to her neck. Sharp pain traveled a path down her neck to her collarbone. "I'll carve you so you bleed slow." The pain continued across her collarbone, and downward, until she felt the knife slashing at the top of her jeans.

Death would not be in time. She would have to endure this. The sharp edge of a zipper raked across the tender skin of her inner thigh. She could no longer tell the exact places where the knife had been. Pain was everywhere. But she would not go on their terms. She would find her place of peace first. She would block the pain, refuse them the power. Quickly her mind searched through space and time to catch sight of her. Swooping in large circles through open spaces of time, speeding faster and faster, feeling the urgency of the search. There, she was there, on the hill; wind blowing the wavy mane of dark hair behind her, head lifted to the sky. NaNan's warrior, just as she remembered her. Sage closed her eyes to make the vision clearer. Stoic and proud, the woman

33

stood, preparing for battle. Arms, outstretched in receiver-ship, welcomed the ancient *orenda*, sought the calm and the strength for her spirit. With her mind, Sage did the same. Opened her arms to *orenda*, accepted the spirit within, becoming one with the warrior. Her body relaxed in resolution, placid in her place of peace. Metabolized in analgesic spirit, she felt no pain.

"Jesus, Bobby. Hurry up."

"Fuck! The bitch passed out." He delivered a forceful slap to her face, but there was no reaction. "Come on, bitch, you're gonna feel this."

The man holding her down released her right arm. There was the sound of another zipper. "Get up, Bobby," he said, "I'm doing her." He flipped open his belt buckle as he righted himself. Then came the distinctive sound of solid metal hitting the concrete.

Sage swiftly swept her hand across the ground above her head and found the dropped gun. Without hesitation, she brought it to bear on the face of the man on top of her, and fired. His head snapped back, eyes wide with terror. As his body slumped forward, she fired twice at the running figure of the second man.

With her strength draining fast, she pushed two and three times against the thick, convulsing body on top of her. It finally rolled off of her and flopped onto the concrete. With a gurgling gasp, the body stopped moving, expressionless eyes staring at the stars they could no longer see. It was done.

Weak and covered in her own blood, she tried to take a deep breath. She felt nothing. She had risen above the pain and had escaped death. And now, as long as her spirit would allow, she would fight to stay alive. Sage set her jaw. Unsteadily, she rolled to her right, resting her weight on her forearm. She must stand. She attempted to pull her legs under her, but they shook uncontrollably. The extent of her numbness surprised her. She could feel the concrete only with her hands. Her body seemed incapable of meeting her command.

Yet her spirit would not be denied. Over and over, she pushed upward in an attempt to stand. Each time, weakened legs refused the weight, shaking convulsively. Relentlessly, she began again. At last her spirit persevered. On legs, so unstable they almost buckled twice, Sage Bristo stood. She straightened tall, held out her arms, and tilted her face to the sky.

The world went dark.

Pat's voice echoed in the darkness. Someone was holding her hand. "Goddamn it, Sage. Don't you dare leave me. Do you hear me? Hang on, damn it!"

Sage turned toward the voice and opened her eyes. Pat's face and worried eyes met hers. "I called Cimmie. She'll meet us at the hospital."

Sage closed her eyes and squeezed her hand.

Chapter 7

Pat hurried down the hallway of the intensive care unit to catch Cimmie before she entered the room. "Cim, I'm sorry. I'm so sorry." She clutched Cimmie's hand with a death-like grip. "I should have apologized last night but things were so harried."

"It's all—"

"I'm such an asshole. For one more dance with a redhead who forgot my name five minutes later, I let Sage take off alone."

"She's going to be okay, Pat. It's not pretty, but she'll be fine." Cimmie placed her free hand over Pat's tight hold. "Don't blame yourself. You know Sage well enough to know that she doesn't depend on anyone else for anything. She never expected you to leave with her. When she's more with it, she'll tell you that herself."

"Is she awake?"

"It's hard to tell."

They entered the room where Sage lay in a slightly propped position with her eyes closed.

"She does this thing I've never been able to understand," Cimmie continued. "She's tried to explain it so many times, but I don't think I'll ever comprehend it. Something my grandmother taught her. She shuts out everything around her, kind of like a dream state I think, and in her mind she becomes this warrior." She looked at Pat who was staring at the blood-soaked bandages that started below Sage's ear and disappeared under the sheet covering Sage's chest.

"I know it sounds crazy, but somehow she takes on the warrior's strength and then she doesn't feel the pain."

"I'm sure they pumped her full of pain-killer when they stitched her up."

Cimmie nodded. "But they would have worn off hours ago. The nurse keeps telling me to push the button when she starts getting uncomfortable, but she hasn't even opened her eyes."

Pat placed her hand on the sheet next to Sage's arm. "Whatever works, pal," she said quietly. Then she squeezed Cimmie's hand more gently this time. "I won't disturb her. When she wakes up tell her I'll be back after work."

Trees, variegated green and full-leafed, were still against an endless, azure dimension. The pure, sweet scents of wild phlox and chicory mingled and rode the currents of air over the hillside where the warrior napped. She rested, safely hidden in the tall grasses, no scent of danger to disturb her peace, no sounds except the buzz of the locusts. Her mind, like her body, was at peace here. There would be time enough later for tracking and hunting — time for gathering courage, time for battle. For there would be another battle, and the length of her life, she knew, depended always on her preparation for the next battle. Now, though, was the time for healing.

Something warm touched her hand and a soft voice told the warrior, "Oh, no, no, your work is not done. So much more to do, so much more to see."

Molly rubbed a warm thick hand over the slenderness of Sage's as Sage opened her eyes. "Ah, there you are, sweet girl," she said with a squeeze. "It's just ol' Molly come to keep you company."

Sage spoke just above a whisper. "How did you get here?"

"You'd be surprised how inconspicuous a cabbie can be for an extra ten dollars."

Sage smiled despite the short twinges of pain that were beginning to shoot down her neck.

"Can't remember you ever missing a day of work. It only took you being gone one day for the rumors to go flying all over Westbrooke. But I've never been one to trust what's come through so many people. I had to come see for myself that you're all right."

"You think this is a little drastic to get a couple of vacation days out of them?"

Molly's giggle was light and girlish. "There, now I know; you're just fine. Are they treating you right at this resort?"

The pain was more pronounced, but Sage's voice gained strength. "I don't know what I was thinking. Lousy room service, no pool."

"Not much better than Westbrooke."

"But you can leave . . . with the right cabbie."

"How long are they going to keep you?"

"Too long if it's left up to my sister." She managed to contain what would have been an obvious grimace and stopped the urge for what would surely have been a painful stretch of her body. "I'll give her another day, then I'll have to pull big-sister rank."

"No such thing as rank in a place like this. Might as well know that early. Need is a common denominator," she said with a slow shake of her head, "and pain is a fierce equalizer. They leave you with few choices. But you're lucky that you're young and strong. You won't be here long."

"I *will* have a choice, as long as I can walk."

Molly nodded. "You exercise those choices as long as you have them. One day you'll look for them and they'll be gone."

"I was already there once, that place of no choice. I'll never be there again. There are always choices, Molly, no matter how small, no matter how imperfect. If there was nothing else that I learned from my parents it was that — even bad choices give you control."

Molly watched her for many seconds, uninterrupted, comfortable in Sage's gaze. Finally she gave a quick nod of her head and spoke. "We're not afraid to learn from each other, you and I."

"Isn't that why we're here?"

"Yes, it is. It certainly is." She paused again, her eyes narrowing but never leaving Sage's. "I *do* have a choice — not a perfect one for sure. And I dismissed it because of that. I wanted to live close to most of my family, and that meant living at Westbrooke."

She needed to say no more. "You're going to Virginia," Sage said as a smile eased into place.

"My granddaughter," Molly confirmed, "The one who reminds me a little of you. She asked me again yesterday to come. She says she wants to learn to garden."

"She wants you in her life or she wouldn't keep asking."

"She's a good girl, always keeps in touch with the rest of the family. Calls me three or four times a week. No husband, no kids, but she has a busy life."

"Coaches youth soccer."

"You don't forget. I never have to wonder with you if you're placating or really listening."

Some things just naturally stick in one's memory. "I'll miss you, Molly. Will she bring you on holidays?"

Molly nodded. "Can we keep our friendship by phone?"

"Can and will." She motioned toward her cell phone on the bedside cabinet just out of reach. "That's the furthest it's been from my hand."

Molly leaned back, picked up the phone and placed it on the bed next to Sage's hand. "In case I don't get the chance again to say this face to face, I want you to know that I love you."

Despite the pain it caused, Sage nodded carefully. "It's important to be able to say what's in you heart, and so I tell you, too, that I love you, Molly Berger."

Chapter 8

Pacifying the doctor proved easier than Sage anticipated. After three days all she had to do was accept the prescription, promise to stay down, and not to go to work until he released her. Cimmie, however, was a different story. If she hadn't consented to stay at Cimmie's, her sister would have parked herself in Sage's apartment and not left until *she* was satisfied that all was well. But what surprised Sage was that her body, with its massive bruises and multiple stitches, hurt so badly that she actually allowed Cimmie to take care of her for two and a half weeks.

Pat stopped by almost every day, partly out of love and concern, partly out of guilt for having allowed her to leave alone that night.

The deep purple of the bruises had begun to fade into softer hues of pink and yellow. The stitches had dissolved. Only the emotional wounds remained. She would have to make them, too, into scars; something her battle-worn psyche already had plenty of. John Jeremy Capra had seen to that. She had earned her scars just being a child, incapable of understanding the unreasonable demands and raging temper of the man she knew as her father. Not even the birth of his son, the ultimate requirement he'd made of his wife, made life easier for the sisters. Jeremy, the chosen one with strong Italian features so like his father, would carry on the family name. John Capra raised him in accordance to his perceived worth, creating many new demands, and thus many more possibilities for shortcomings by the sisters. Even separation did not stop the torment, for it meant not seeing Cimmie, and unrelenting guilt for having left her alone. Only through the clever schemes of her grandmother were the sisters able to be together. Any slipup would result in severe punishment for Cimmie; a liability Sage carried always.

"My attorney called today." She directed the news at Cimmie, busily cooking their dinner. "We finally have a hearing date on NaNan's will."

"When?"

"Thursday. Her exact words were, 'We have John Jeremy by the scrotum.' She sounds very confident."

"I hope so, Sage. This thing needs to be over." She stopped stirring momentarily to look at her sister. "There is no one on earth more deserving of that money than you."

"At first, it was only to keep the money out of his hands that I fought. But, I've come to realize how important it was to NaNan that I have it." She took the spoon from Cimmie, and began to stir. "You know, I never took a cent of her money for school. She kept trying to pay my tuition, but I worked all those overtime hours and paid it all myself. It wasn't until she died that I realized how important it was. If I had allowed her, I could have had so much more time with her. That's all she really wanted. What she valued was our time together and me. What good is the money to her now? What good is it to me? I can't buy back that time."

"Retrospective vision can make geniuses out of morons," Cimmie said, reclaiming the spoon and motioning for Sage to sit. "You made what you felt was an unselfish decision at the time. Don't feel guilty about that."

"Today, for the first time, I seriously thought about what I would do with the money. I've decided on some things that I think NaNan would be proud to be a part of." Cimmie began serving simmered stew and homemade bread. "I'm going to establish an educational fund for Seneca girls. And I'm going to develop a retirement community for the old ones that society treats so disrespectfully so that they can live with safety and dignity."

"Oh, Sage. What a wonderful idea." Cimmie carefully wrapped her arms around her sister's still tender shoulders and kissed her cheek.

"It'll have to be just the right location, with ample grounds for planting and gardens, and space for workshops and social gatherings. I know what NaNan needed to feel in control of her life, to feel vital. I want to be able to provide that. Neither of the facilities I've worked in offer the quality of life I know is possible."

"I can't think of a more suitable investment." Cimmie enjoyed Sage's most beautiful smile; a rarity in recent months. It made her heart glad to see the joy the idea brought her. She hoped it wasn't just a prelude to more disappointment.

"I'm going back to work tomorrow." They split another piece of bread. "I need to get out of your hair so that Jeff can stop being so courteous and spend the night with you. And I need to start figuring out how I'm going to repay you."

Cimmie rested her elbows on the edge of the table and stared into Sage's eyes. She shook her head. "After all the times in my life that you've been my heroine? I think not." She hesitated with an understanding smile. "You're getting stir-crazy aren't you?" Sage nodded. "This means you're well enough to start the therapy sessions, too."

"A sadistic order."

"Realistically, they may never catch the other guy. The best the court can do is to insure that you have the help you need to deal with what's happened."

"How can reliving it over and over, in the presence of a stranger, possibly help? What's the point? It's sadistic."

"It's not a choice."

Chapter 9

"No, she could not have lived some of the stories herself," testified Ben Silverhorn. Dressed in a three-piece suit, mostly graying hair tied neatly behind his neck, he hardly looked the part of a tribal sachem. Yet, he was proving to be the perfect expert witness to the origin of NaNan's folklore, and thus to her sanity. "But, she was not imagining them either. I helped trace her lineage through the Hodinon'/deogg', the clan of the doe, as far back as we could. She spent her childhood, as had much of her family before her, on the Seneca reservation at Allegheny. But it was still not an easy task. Indian names became Americanized over the years. Plus Iroquois descent is maintained by the woman's name, not the man's. So when Iroquois women married white men, the lineage became con-

45

fused, and many times lost. Without Ms. Bristo's incredible memory, we could not have gone past the third generation."

"You're saying that the clans in the longhouses, and the battles she described, were not things she actually witnessed herself?" Attorney D'Armon was right to the point and getting quickly to the heart of his information, which was exactly why Sage had chosen her.

"That's correct. Only through pictures and a vivid memory of the old one's stories."

"And by 'old one's,' to whom are you referring?"

"Storytellers and elders of the clan. Much of Indian history has been passed from generation to generation through stories or verbal accounts. It has proven to be most reliable, since so many recorded accounts have been lost. Their accuracy has stood up against even modern-day challenges."

"So, in a sense, NaNan Bristo was merely doing her part to hand down her heritage, the legacy of her people, to another generation."

"Yes, that's correct. When her own daughter was disinterested and alienated, she passed it to a receptive granddaughter."

"Am I correct then, in concluding that in your expert opinion, the stories related by NaNan Bristo were not the crazy ramblings of a senile old woman?"

"They were not."

"Thank you, Mr. Silverhorn."

Almost immediately, the large heavy man seated next to John Capra pushed back his chair and rose. "Mr. Silverhorn, do you believe in evil spirits?"

"Yes, I do."

"How about inanimates, Mr. Silverhorn. Do they have spirits?"

"Inanimates?"

"Wind, trees, water."

"Yes."

"Do the spirits talk to you, Mr. Silverhorn?"

"Well . . ."

The attorney's voice rose a level. "Have the spirits ever talked to you?"

The sachem cleared his throat and readjusted his position. "Yes, but —"

"Thank you. That's all."

Sage whispered quickly in the ear of her attorney. "May I have a moment, Your Honor?" She acknowledged his go ahead, and gave attention to her client. A moment later, she rose and strode pensively in front of the table. "Mr. Silverhorn, can you explain to us more clearly what the Iroquois, ergo you, believe in regard to spirits?"

"Yes, thank you." He directed his attention now to Judge Kendall. "I'll try to be as concise as I can." He cleared his throat once again. "The Iroquois believe that each person is filled with a spirit that connects one another and to an overall force. You may have heard that force called the Great Spirit. The Iroquois refer to a spirit we call *orenda*. It may be easier for you to think of *orenda* as similar to God and Holy Spirit of the Christian religion. *Orenda*, if respected and honored, brings unity to the Indian people and harmony with all of the world around them." He made a gesture with his thick hands, encompassing the air before him. "The time we are at rest is the time we are most receptive to our Spirit." The lines surrounding his dark eyes deepened into a gentle smile. "That is why we pay close attention to remembering and analyzing our dreams. Through them we gain advice and guidance for our lives."

"You made analogies to the Christian religion. Have you, in fact, just described your religion to us?"

"Yes, without going into a lot of detail, that is the basis of the Longhouse religion. But, it's important to know that the Indian does not separate religion from other parts of their life or even apply religion to their life. Their religion is their life. It is generally not spoken of in separate terms."

"This will be my last question, Your Honor." Ms.

47

D'Armon's efficiency ran from her simple dark suit to her courtroom manner, an attribute greatly appreciated in Judge Kendall's court. "Is it your understanding that NaNan Bristo held that same religion or belief?"

"Yes, it is."

"Thank you, Mr. Silverhorn. Your Honor, we have nothing further."

Judge Kendall turned his attention fully to John Capra's attorney. "Mr. Gionni, anything further?"

"No, Your Honor."

"Very well. I am not inclined to deliberate any further on this matter." Judge Kendall looked sternly at the severe-looking man, who sat so straight before him. "Mr. Capra, I suggest that you find another cause to spend your money on. This time, one that will in some way be of benefit to mankind. This matter has been far too long in coming to this court and to fruition." He relaxed his furrowed brow when he turned to the table on the other side of the room.

"Ms. Bristo," he began. "Please accept the apology of this court for what seems to be one of the shortcomings of an otherwise irreplaceable system of justice. It may be of little comfort to you, but the very things that make this system the best in the world also make it vulnerable to abuses."

Sage nodded her understanding.

"This court finds in favor of Ms. Bristo. The last will and testament of NaNan Bristo will stand as written." Then, with a quick thwack of his gavel, he sealed the decision that had been so long in coming.

Sage looked across the room at John Capra. Her expression was one of glib finality; his was one of seething anger. He had tried it all, exhausted every legal maneuver, found every excuse for delay. Yet it had not worn her down. She had proved to be a formidable opponent, and he had lost.

For years now, the only hold he had, the last tie that forced her to recognize his existence, had been NaNan's will. The decision whether to fight for what her grandmother wanted or simply to let it go had been difficult. But once made, she never varied from it. It was finally over. She was free of him and his haunting hatred at last.

"Congratulations, Sage." Lyn D'Armon extended her hand.

"Thank you."

"It's been my pleasure. Winning a judgment against that man makes me remember why I'm in this profession."

The sisters walked the hall together after the initial flow from the courtroom had passed. Only a trickle of people occupied the hallway. An emotional Cimmie embraced Sage warmly. "I'm so happy for you. You're free now."

Sage nodded, squeezing her gratefully in return. "Thanks for being here. It's always meant a lot to me."

Behind them, the courtroom door thrust open, banging loudly against the wall. Accompanying its startling echo, John Capra burst into the hallway. Lena Capra dutifully followed an arm's distance behind him. He stormed toward the sisters, anger evident in every step. "Get your hands off her," he shouted. "You're nothing but a sick pervert."

Sage moved away from Cimmie but stood her ground as her father threateningly closed the distance. His presence, although not nearly so foreboding as in her childhood, was nonetheless intimidating. She matched his height now; her eyes were level with his, and every bit as unsparing. Blood engorged the large vein crossing his temple, his cheeks quivered, telltale signs of his struggle to stay in control.

"It's time to walk away and let it be," she calmly advised.

"You're disgusting, spreading your sickness wherever you go," he spat.

"Leave her alone," Cimmie ordered, restrained by Sage's arm from moving any closer.

"I had to protect you from her all these years," he directed at Cimmie, "to keep her from touching you, from forcing her sickness on you."

Cimmie's voice rose noticeably. "You succeeded in doing nothing but making me hate you."

"Cimmie! Don't ever speak to your father that way." Her daughter's new strength surprised the predictably dutiful and supportive Lena Capra.

"There are a lot of things I should have said years ago." Her eyes zeroed in with a pointed finger at her father. "You are the only sickness in this family — you and a mother whose weakness nursed it."

John Capra moved menacingly forward, met squarely by a defiant Sage. "Your problem, big man, is with me." His eyes went back to her and met the chill of her stare. "You're dealing with a woman now; not a child. And not a subservient wife you can control."

"You're not a woman." He spat with increased agitation. "You're nothing, a profanity. What you do to women is a desecration."

There was a sinister curl to the corners of Sage's mouth as she spoke. "What I do to women, you can only dream about. I touch them in ways you'll never know, until they demand my lips, my mouth, until they scream my name in ecstasy."

"Whores!" he shouted, striking her across the face with such force that it snapped her head sharply to one side.

"No, no more!" shouted Cimmie. Sage held her position, and held out a protective arm to prevent her sister from moving any closer.

Sage had never raised her hand to their father, nor even her voice. The only thing she had ever raised was the truth, the cold, biting truth. It was much more effective, and inflicted much more pain. "No, not whores," she said, her glare finding his eyes once more. "Beautiful women, married to men like you —"

"Sage, stop!" Cimmie pleaded.

She persisted. "Selfish, ignorant men, incapable of loving women."

Control gone, he raised his hand swiftly to strike again. This time, Sage grabbed it by the wrist, sinking her fingers into the sleeve of the other arm as well. Her strength shocked him. With restrained anger she warned, "Don't you ever touch me again."

"Or what?" he growled. "You'll shoot me?"

With surprising force, she pushed him back away from her. "Are you willing to find out?"

Tearfully, Lena pleaded, "Please, John."

"Stop whimpering and go to the car," he ordered.

Cimmie took Sage's arm and eased her back out of range. "Come on, it's over now. It's over. Please, Sage. Let's get out of here."

They left him standing in the middle of the hallway, alone, as he would always be, with his ignorance and his anger. She had won her lifelong battle to be free of him. Yes, this time, it really was over.

Chapter 10

The sign on the semi-cluttered desk read Joyce Gilbert, Psy. D. Sage stood behind the brown tweed chair obviously intended for the client and surveyed the office. Photo prints of some of the city's finest attractions hung alongside numerous professional certificates on a wallpapered wall. Professional books and periodicals lined the ledge of the large window behind her. There were no personal pictures on the desk or file cabinet. No indication of a life outside the office walls. Sage wondered how someone with so little personal connection to life could have the skills necessary to pull intimate details from the minds of her clients. She was skeptical.

"Ms. Bristo." A portly bespectacled woman, dressed in a

skirt and long jacket, extended her hand. "I'm Dr. Gilbert. I apologize for the wait. Information doesn't always make it to my desk as fast as I'd like. Please have a seat."

Sage eased gracefully into the tweed chair and crossed her legs at the knee.

"I understand you had some physical problems. I hope you're feeling better."

"Yes."

"Wonderful, wonderful. And, you're back to work now?"

"Yes."

"Good. I'm sure you're finding that helpful." Dr. Gilbert relaxed against the back of her chair. "I appreciate that you have to leave work early. What do you do?"

"I'm an administrative assistant at a large retirement facility."

"Do you enjoy it?"

"It'll do for now."

"What do you like to do for enjoyment?"

"I ride horses and drive fast cars."

Obviously unable to relate to those particular activities, Dr. Gilbert continued. "Personally, I enjoy old movies and professional football." She laughed and shook her head. "Quite a combination. I'm sure a number of my colleagues have had fun with that. Are you a sports fan?"

"Not since Martina retired."

Dr. Gilbert smiled and nodded. "She certainly kept things exciting for a long time. I guess I never thought the time would come when she wouldn't play."

Sage acknowledged the first connection between them and wondered if the doctor thought something so trivial could actually gain her access.

The remainder of their first session consisted of more seemingly insignificant questions. Sage's brief answers offered no details and little insight. She found herself trying to decide whether her irritation was a result of the strategy being so obvious, or of the session being such a waste of time. Dr. Gilbert seemed undaunted. Predictably so. After all, she earned the same amount of money regardless.

Personal questions in the beginning of the second session nudged close to the edge of Sage's comfort zone. It was not unlike the feeling of picking off the dried edges of a large scab, and coming too close to the not quite healed center. The process was illogical. Why tear the scab off a successfully closed wound? Where was the healing value in that, in feeling the pain again? Hadn't she successfully made wounds into scars for years now? Certainly Dr. Gilbert wasn't proposing that she could make the wound disappear without a scar.

"You know, Ms. Bristo, you and I are destined to live out the duration of the court-ordered sessions. It's standard practice in cases like this. But if we're going to get anywhere, I'm going to need your cooperation."

Sage's steely eyes, devoid of emotion, never left Dr. Gilbert's. "Don't you suppose it would help if I knew where it was we were supposed to go?"

"I need to know what your feelings are at this point in order to help you through the healing process." As she was speaking, Sage left her seat. She slowly paced the length of the large window, gazing silently at the city. "I have very little to go on, except assumptions, unless you help me." Dr. Gilbert waited, watching the abstinence in the set of her shoulders, the hold of her head. The hard set of the masseter muscle defined her jaw. "Maybe it would help if we started with the facts, as they were presented to me." The silent figure remained stoic. "You were attacked. You sustained knife wounds from fighting back. You ended up shooting and killing one of your attackers with their own gun. Are my facts correct?"

"Exactly."

"Past those facts, you are leaving me with only assumptions, assumptions that may or may not be true. The accuracy of my evaluation will be greatly affected by the correctness of those assumptions." She hesitated for a response but got none. "For instance, what assumption should I draw from the fact that you were attacked around the corner from a gay bar?" She waited patiently.

"Why don't you assume that I'm a lesbian. Will that make it easier?"

"Somewhat. It's important that you be honest with me. That's a good place to start . . .You know, many experts tell you to fight back, unless there's a weapon involved. You faced two weapons and still fought. Were *you* making an assumption?"

"That I was dead regardless? Yes."

"That had to have been a tough decision to make."

Arms folded across her chest, Sage turned toward Dr. Gilbert and leaned against the windowsill. "Have you ever been raped?"

The reversal surprised her. Dr. Gilbert adjusted her glasses and leaned back in her chair. "No."

"Abused?"

"No." She knew where this was going now.

"Are you a lesbian, Dr. Gilbert?"

"Yes." There was no hesitation in her answer. She smiled at her client's stare. "You were about to rest your case, weren't you?"

The edges of Sage's mouth turned up almost unnoticeably. "Touché." She watched Dr. Gilbert tip an imaginary hat in acknowledgment. "That accounts for the lack of family pictures on the desk." Sage placed her hands back on the windowsill and appeared more at ease. "Can I assume, then, that I won't be insulted with antiquated theory that ties my sexuality to childhood abuse and a hatred of men?"

"You may," she smiled. "I believe, very strongly, that we

are born with our sexuality, leaving the identification of it as the main issue. Our society still makes it practically impossible for young children to have positive gay role models. That makes clear and comfortable identification extremely difficult, and many times unnecessarily dangerous." Dr. Gilbert watched Sage nod in agreement, the first positive response in two sessions. "Any child, gay or straight, male or female, black or white, is going to react with predictable certainty to abuse. And the same goes for reactions to sexual assault and violence as adults. All humans are going to react with behaviors that have been documented for years, with very few exceptions. To say that lesbians and gay males seek out their own gender as a result is absurd at best."

Sage tilted her head ever so slightly, just enough to indicate resolution. "You've completely shattered my perception of shrinks."

"Well, I asked for honesty," Dr Gilbert laughed. "I think it's going to surprise you how easy it will be to explore even the most private parts of your soul with me. You will be talking to someone who has formed no opinion of you as a person, who will make no judgments of your thoughts, and who is professionally bound by confidentiality. Who, besides a gay pastor, would be safer?"

"I don't see how it can be of any help to relive the pain. I've put it behind me; it serves no constructional purpose. I've already moved on." Ultimately, she knew, she would simply have to tell the good doctor what she wanted to hear.

"If you've truly done that, you've had practice."

"Years of it."

"Abuse?"

"Physically and emotionally."

"Not sexually?"

"No."

"Was the abuse by your father?"

Sage turned again to look at the city. "Yes, but my mother isn't totally blameless."

"Was she afraid of him?"

"Still is. She's a weak woman. I have no respect for her."

"Have you told her how you feel?"

"As a young girl." She turned back to Dr. Gilbert. "I lived with my grandmother from age eleven."

"So you've never told her as an adult."

Sage shook her head slowly. "I learned very early to let go of things I couldn't change."

"If, in fact, you have that ability, it's remarkable. But I'd like you to at least consider confronting your parents here, one at a time, of course."

"Even in the remote chance that they would show up, what could possibly be accomplished? My father would erupt in anger, my mother in guilt-ridden tears. It's totally unreasonable."

Dr. Gilbert leaned forward on her elbows, placing the palms of her hands together and interlacing her fingers. "In a controlled setting, these kinds of confrontations have proven quite beneficial. The presence of a trained intermediary can make all the difference. It provides a safe place for you to tell the other person exactly how you feel, and in turn hear their feelings. It's often the first step in beginning to understand each other."

After a deep breath, which always helped her composure and patience, Sage offered her last explanation. "In order for something like that to occur, there would have to be a willingness, or at least a reason, for both parties to try. It is not possible in this case. They have disowned me, and I want nothing more to do with them. To spend even minutes in thought over it is a terrible waste of time, not unlike these sessions." Once again she straightened her body and steeled her stare.

Undaunted, Dr. Gilbert leaned back comfortably in her chair. "If nothing else, you'll find it comforting to be able to tell me anything you want. You don't have to worry about how you say it. You can't lose a friendship over it or hurt my feelings. Where else can you do that?"

Chapter 11

Despite carefully self-constructed blinds that protected her client's deepest feelings, Dr. Gilbert peered through the camouflage that hid the scars and walked fearlessly through the minefields of Sage Bristo's emotions. She penetrated the fortress, came close enough to recognize the pain, and began to comfort it.

Trickles of personal facts soon became a flood of painful information flowing through the breaks in the fortress. Sage finally released the secrets of abuse she and Cimmie had kept between them for years. She talked of nearly crippling beatings, dark closets, and extended periods without food or bathroom privileges. She told of the lonely cries of a frightened little girl, and the soft little hand of her sister sliding under the door, braving further wrath just to touch her fingers. Her only physical comfort.

She talked session after session, unfolding bad dreams, unleashing hidden guilt for having left her sister alone. Then unleashing anger, in all its rawness, at her father and her mother. And finally at her attackers and the reason why she was there, the almost unbearable anger . . . and murder without guilt.

Who the attackers were didn't matter. Why they attacked her didn't even matter. That it happened, despite her best efforts at disempowering the act, did matter. It mattered because her right to feel safe was important, because her right to be happy was important, and it mattered because she was important. And no one, not a stranger, not her father, had the right to destroy that for her.

Had revenge, partial as it was, dispelled some of her rage? Maybe. She was grateful for even a partial sense of justice. So many suffer with no justice at all for their pain. Yes, it did help to know he couldn't do it again. And the rest of her anger? She would handle it with resolve, as she always had, having vented what she could with Dr. Gilbert. Only one thing would change. She would no longer ignore her constitutional right to bear arms.

"You realize this is the last time you have to come and talk to me?" Dr. Gilbert was saying. "My determination is that you have a surprisingly healthy psyche, despite , as you say, the 'nasty hand' life dealt you. I want you to remember that healing is a lifelong process. There will be times when the twists and turns of life will make the process easier, and times they will make it more difficult. I'm here if you want to come back and talk or unload," she said with a smile. "Are you comfortable with dealing with the bad dreams?"

"I can see now how leaving the bedroom door open and being able to see a light prevents them. I've never had a nightmare when I've fallen asleep with my arms around someone."

"It's important to consciously understand those connections, however simplistic it seems. Your unconscious mind has already made those connections. They can show up in dreams and unexplained reactions to seemingly unrelated situations. Just identifying and understanding the connection are vital steps toward eliminating the reactions."

"Even someone as obstinate as I can appreciate how much that's helped."

"Remember, occasional nightmares or reactionary fear of someone grabbing you from behind, or even grabbing you playfully, are normal reactions. They could be around for some time."

"At least I don't have to deal with a boyfriend or husband."

"Yes, but you may experience a feeling of resistance to being touched intimately even by a woman. If you normally receive sexually, as well as give, you may have to be patient with yourself for a while. Usually, time and the right person do as much to help in bringing about normalcy as anything. But if you need me, I'm at the other end of the phone."

Sage smiled and extended her hand. "Was I the most insolent client you've ever had?"

"Actually, you're one of the brightest and most interesting, a challenge that snatched me up from my boredom. I do wish we could have met under happier conditions, but then I wouldn't have gotten to know you so well." She released Sage's hand and walked her to the door. "One last piece of advice." — her eyes took on a soft maternal quality — "don't give up on love. It can be as wonderful as it is painful."

Chapter 12

Sage placed another box on the stack next to the door of NaNan's kitchen. Each box was clearly labeled by contents and sizes. NaNan's clothing, all washed and ironed, would go to her Westbrooke residents. For the first time in four years Sage had stepped legally onto her grandmother's property, *her* property now.

After all this time the process was finally underway, but she was finding it to be a difficult and painful one. In many ways the years of limbo had been easier. She didn't have to make the tough decisions because they weren't legally hers to make. But now it was time and Sage had begun where she could, with the easy decisions first. The bureau drawers were empty, the closets cleared of everything except the boxes of things that NaNan had saved over the years. Every card and gift that Sage had ever given her, every paper or school project she had brought home was there. Sage knelt among the boxes in the bedroom that had been hers for so many years. *So this is where everything ended up after they disappeared from the refrigerator magnets and bureau top.* "I shouldn't be surprised, sweet lady."

She continued looking through the contents, stopping here and there to read childhood birthday wishes and holiday greetings. Some she remembered, some she didn't. The next one she could have given yesterday. She pulled it from the pile. It was a Father's Day card with the word *Father* crossed out and *Parent* written above it. She didn't need the date on the inside to tell her the year. Her thirteenth year had been a memorable one. It was the year that the tug-of-war had ended. Protective love had won out over pretense and duty. Her mother had finally decided to risk whatever anyone else had to say about NaNan raising her troubled daughter in trade for a more comfortable life with her husband. Without Sage, Cimmie was manageable. Unquestioning, obedient, and easily intimidated, she was less likely to test her husband's patience and incite his fury. And with her son holding special favor in his father's eyes, life was just easier.

Without realizing it, Sage had left her bedroom, walked the length of the hall and settled on the side of her grandmother's bed. The card was still in her hand. She opened it again and read aloud.

"There are many kinds of greatness in this world . . .
But yours — which comes from your wisdom, strength, warmth and courage — makes you exceptional and very special to me."

The message was so much a part of her heart that even at thirteen the card had been an obvious choice. She had always feared that her own words would not be adequate, that they would not be beautiful enough to say what she felt. Although she always signed each card with *I love you. Thank you for loving me,* it wasn't until now that she realized the impact that those words coming from a teenager must have had on her grandmother. Sage picked up her grandmother's pillow, pressed it to her face and breathed deeply. But it had been too long; her scent was gone.

Love, she had finally come to understand, really couldn't be defined by words; it was in the living of it that it was told. Like religion was lived, so was love. It manifested itself everyday of her life here. Because of its presence, Sage had listened and learned, had spoken and been heard. She had respected and had been respected in return, had needed yet never had to want. Within these walls she had flourished and grown in both stature and character. Love had made it her home.

Now it was just a house. Its walls were covered with pictures and memories, its rooms only space for a life that no longer needed it. Gone the way of her grandmother's spirit were the sounds and the smells that had given her comfort here. Gone and irreplaceable was the person who had known her better than any other. And staying here wouldn't bring any of it back.

Sage looked around the room. It had changed very little through the years. The wallpaper with its tiny purple violets, the mahogany bureau and the old flattop trunk with the wampum belt draped across it had always been there. The round-faced clock that Sage still kept faithfully wound ticked softly on the beside stand. This was a room that was as familiar to her as her own. It had been a place of sharing, where family history and Seneca tradition was told over pictures and cherished artifacts. Cuddled against the pillows and her grandmother's side, she had listened to life's lessons folded discreetly within the stories that had been passed from generation to generation. And here was where she slept, wrapped in the safety of her grandmother's arms, when nightmares filled her with terror.

"What would you have me do?" Sage whispered. She walked around the bed, her hand following the smooth curve of the wood of the footboard. *Would you understand if I sold it?* "God, I don't even know if I could." *Not right now. It wouldn't have to be right away. Maybe in time. Maybe someday if I ever have a house of my own.*

Sage opened the lid of a small wooden box on the bureau. Lovingly she fingered each of the pieces inside, then lifted a colorful braided bracelet and squeezed it over her hand to her wrist. She followed it with a black leather rope bracelet and then added a silver braid next to that. In the bottom of the box was the broken silver necklace that she had promised to fix years ago. She picked it out, wound it around her wrist and fastened it together with the clasp of the silver bracelet. These would be her reminders, along with the memories pressed within her heart, that she had once been loved.

Chapter 13

"Cim, I'm going to look at another property," Sage said, enjoying their first Saturday in weeks together.

"I'm glad you're not getting frustrated. You've looked at so many."

"So far, each property has had faults so glaring, I'm not even tempted. Either the location wasn't close enough to a city, or if it was, it was too small for individual units, or it was just plain ugly. I know exactly what I want. I'll just have to keep looking. This next one . . ." She hesitated until Cimmie raised her eyes. "This one's out of state . . . Michigan."

"Michigan?!" It did take Cimmie by surprise. She hadn't realized the extent to which Sage was willing to go.

"I know it's kind of a shock, and it might not be anything.

I wanted to prepare you in case it does turn out to be a serious possibility."

"How did you find out about it?"

"Pat's from Michigan. Some weeks ago she mentioned to a friend that I was looking. That friend sent her some information on a piece of property not far from her. It sounds interesting enough to warrant a trip to Michigan. I booked a flight out Friday morning. I'll be back Sunday night."

"And, if it is the one?"

"Then we'll talk again."

"Sage, as much as I love you — and it's more than I've ever been able to put into words — I would never want to feel that I was keeping you from something that would make you happy. For once in your life, you need to make a decision based solely on what Sage Bristo wants. If you do any less, I'll know it."

"You're the only thing that would keep me here."

"That's what I'm telling you. I know that."

"I would miss you terribly . . . and I would worry."

"And I would miss you, and probably have to make a gazillion trips to Michigan. But to know you're unhappy, would be much worse."

"Are you and Jeff pretty solid?"

"Any relationship that can successfully endure your loving but relentless scrutiny must be pretty solid."

Sage matched Cimmie's smile. "He knows the rules pretty well, doesn't he?"

Cimmie laughed. "Yes, dear sister, you've taught him the rules well. Unconditional love, absolute respect, uncompromising fidelity; nothing less will be tolerated."

Sage responded with an easy nod. She had to admit, she liked Jeff; not many guys qualified for that statement.

"I want the same thing for you too, you know. Maybe I should be so bold as to scrutinize your women. Although, at times, I'm afraid that may be a full-time job."

"I'm not sure the same kind of commitment is even possible in my life, at least from what I've seen so far." There was a sad resignation in Sage's voice that signaled doubts she hadn't shared with anyone before. So much of what they had shared as sisters had been unspoken, sensed and felt but never put into words. Some were simply unnecessary. Doubts and fears about her future, about love and happiness, would only worry Cimmie. She saw no sense in doing that. Yet here she was, giving in to the compulsion to say what she had always feared, that she would never again in her life enjoy a home filled with unconditional love.

"Maybe you're looking in all the wrong places, like the old song says." Cimmie read the strange sadness. She wanted so badly to be able to take it away. She wanted to believe there was a woman out there, fated to come into her sister's life, a woman who would love her as deeply and sincerely as she did. "She's out there, Sage. She just hasn't found you yet."

Challenging the sadness with a slight smile, Sage tried to convince Cimmie the emotion was irrelevant. She sipped her soda and pushed the remainder of her dessert across to Cimmie. "I'm not even sure I'd be good at a long-term relationship. I might not even recognize the opportunity."

"When it's right, you'll know it."

Chapter 14

Metro Airport was a bustle of activity, with tired business-people coming home and excited travelers getting a jump on the weekend. Even on a busy Friday, however, it was no LaGuardia. Sage's long swift strides easily overtook people ahead of her who moved closer to the pace of her residents than her own. She excused herself numerous times before realizing how much out of sync her internal timer was. She made a conscious effort to slow it down. With a deep breath she surveyed the baggage claim area for Pat's old college roommate. Stocky, with short brown hair, she had described herself; blue summer jacket with a rainbow triangle pin on the collar. Out and proud. She smiled to herself. *Excellent*.

Scattered pieces of luggage and duffels began to appear

along the belt. Sage divided her attention between looking for her luggage and looking for her hostess. Her black leather garment bag rolled under the plastic flaps. She claimed it immediately, straightening in time to notice a woman in a blue jacket slowly approaching the area. Sage made eye contact and extended her hand. "Sharon Davis?"

"I am. You must be Sage Bristo."

They exchanged a warm handshake and comfortable polite smiles. "I appreciate your hospitality. Pat sends her greetings."

"Pat and I must have walked off the ark together," Sharon laughed. "We've known each other so long. I'm more than happy to help a friend of hers. She'd do the same for me."

Loyalty, it seemed, was one of Sharon's attributes. She was beginning to like this woman already. "Well, it's nice to meet you Sharon."

"Same here. We'd better get movin', though." Sharon quickened her pace some. "The unies out there grow wild hairs when you leave your car unattended for more than a few minutes."

Sage grinned. "Not unlike New York."

"Did you get the additional information I sent you before you left?" asked Sharon, merging the Blazer onto Interstate 94.

"No, just the initial info you sent Pat; forty acres, partially wooded, backing up to a lake."

"I talked to the Realtor. She admits the house has been neglected and needs major upgrading. And there's some quirky condition that the house can't be torn down. There's also a large barn; I think the owners still board a horse there."

"I'm more concerned about the location, actually. It's imperative for the residents to have easy access to the amenities of a small city. Close proximity will make it more comfortable for those who still drive and easier for me to provide shuttle service for the others."

"We can check the distance ourselves, but it's supposed to be less than six miles from Interstate 96, and approximately fifteen minutes from Brighton. Brighton's small, but growing. Are you sure you don't want to settle in and unwind some before we go to the property?"

Sage's manner was polite, but businesslike. "I'd prefer to go directly to the property, if it's not inconvenient."

"No problem. We're on our way."

Softly rolling hills of tall green, separated from the road by a visibly deteriorating wooden fence, stretched to the feet of thickly clumped oak and pine. The car pulled slowly into a long curving drive and was met at the edge of the curve by a curious bay about fifteen hands high. He followed anxiously at a trot as far as the fence would allow him. Looming at the head of the drive was a magnificent old two-story farmhouse; a kindly spindle-rail porch wrapped its south side.

They walked the perimeter of the house and surveyed the land from each vantage point. The barn was a good distance from the house, making it salvageable even with additional construction.

Sharon motioned toward the back acreage. "The drive continues around the barn, and leads back to the lake."

"Let's go."

The tread-worn drive, so overgrown in places it nearly disappeared, led through a field and an area thickly wooded with oak and pine before almost vanishing at the edge of a second field. Sharon slowly followed the indentations. The glassy surface of the lake gradually became visible over the edge of a low grassy ridge.

"Sharon, I'd like to walk from here."

"Okay." Sharon stopped the car just over the ridge and followed Sage on foot a short distance behind.

It was beautiful, secluded and wild. Sage breathed in the fresh cool breeze that danced playfully through her hair and rippled its way across the glassy surface of the lake. As her lungs filled, she felt wonderfully exhilarated. She had an all but irresistible urge to run as fast as she could through the tall grass until exhausted, then fall on her back and watch the magnificence of the clouds float by. She managed to resist, but the feeling made her smile.

"What d'ya think?"

"I think I'd like to speak to the Realtor."

"I think we have company," Sharon laughed.

Sage turned to see the big bay ambling cordially toward her. With instant affection, he leaned the weight of his huge head clumsily against her shoulder. The push caused her to take two steps back and widen her stance to maintain her balance. He nudged her again. She rubbed the big flat plane between his eyes. "Somebody's lonely," she said affectionately to the big brown eye batting its dark brown lash at her.

"I'm going to have a hard time rivaling that welcome."

Sage grinned and rubbed the velvet nose. "Well, this guy doesn't know it, but he's a privileged character. Males are not allowed in my personal space."

"This one never truly enjoyed malehood," Sharon chuckled.

"Probably why we're getting on so famously. Do you have a rope in the car, Sharon?"

"I think so. Let me look."

Sharon produced a length of nylon rope, then watched as Sage fashioned a makeshift halter and rein and fit it over the horse's head.

"I'll meet you back at the house," she said, grabbing the bay's mane and with apparent ease, swinging herself onto his back.

Immediately exercising control, she walked him to the left, to the right, then into a trot in the direction of the house. They rode for a distance while Sage confidently established control. Then deftly, she urged the massive power beneath her into a comfortable gallop. Sage could feel by the thrust of his head the bay's need to stretch his able legs, and sensed in his quick response to her lead his desire to impress her with his strength and speed. She held him just short of it, having him carry her exactly where she directed, keeping his gait true. They traveled effortlessly over the field of tall grass, the wind whipping his mane against her face. The muscles of her legs gripped and moved with the might of his mass, her hands controlling it. She experienced again a feeling so unique and wonderful that it is equaled by none and surpassed by only one. Even the feel of a high-performance engine, surging and testing her control and responsive to her touch, couldn't match it. Only the emotional power, the sensuous feel, of a woman exploding in orgasm against her, transcended it.

They slowed at the edge of the woods. Heavy breathing took in air lushly scented with pine. Horse and rider caught their breath, carefully stepped over slippery roots, and ducked low hanging branches until the coolness of the wooded path opened into warm bright sunshine and the welcome of a wide-open field. With a surge of excitement, they burst into the field, quickly opening stride into a full gallop. Sage opened her rein. They raced wildly past the edge of restraint into exhilarating freedom. Responsibilities were miles away; worries belonged to a different world. Time lost its relevance. Sage Bristo felt wonderful.

They ran and ran, horse and rider, over the land as if they needed to touch every part of it. They continued until exhaustion took them both. When they rested, she stroked the slick sweaty neck of her unexpected host. "Niio, my friend," she said. "Niio."

Breathless and sweaty, the pair ambled leisurely down the drive toward Sharon, who was waiting patiently on the porch steps. "You two must have had a good time." She smiled as she rose. "Who wore whom out?"

Sage laughed easily. "I think we're mutually exhausted." She dismounted and guided the bay with the halter. "You want to walk with us? I have to find a brush in the barn."

"Yeah. Damn, I never figured you for a horsewoman, coming from New York."

"I've spent a lot of my life in the city, but I've ridden since I was eleven. My grandmother taught me to ride. We'd go every weekend when the weather was good."

"They say horses are stupid. But, I'd trust a horse a lot faster than I'd trust most people."

Sage nodded. "They have a wholesome honesty that's rarely possible in humans."

Sharon looked closely at her intriguing new acquaintance. "It probably would have taken me two paragraphs to say what you just said in a sentence. Are you always so concise?"

"I've never really thought about it. I guess so. I always do a quick sort-through with my mind, toss out unnecessary information, and condense the fragments. It helps me focus. Maybe that's why I was always good at cards." She found a brush hanging inside the neglected stall and began brushing down the bay, while Sharon drew him a fresh trough of water.

Sharon had contained her curiosity as long as she could. "What do you think of this place?"

"I like it." Actually, Sage loved it; it was perfect, almost too perfect. She had felt it the moment they'd turned in the drive. The feeling had gotten stronger the more she saw. And the bay was the closest thing to an omen she'd experienced in a long time. Impulsiveness, she knew, had no place in business decisions, but this was not impulsive, it was right. "I want to talk with the Realtor as soon as possible today. I have to be sure I can get the proper zoning needed and find out if there are any variances required. If there are no problems in that respect, I'm prepared to offer a bid today." A bid, she figured, low enough to act as a safeguard to her decision, but high enough to tempt the seller into a cash transaction.

"Are decisions usually made this quickly in New York, or is it that you know exactly what you're looking for?"

"Ever hear of a *New York minute*? It means if you don't think as quick as you blink, your chance is gone. And, yes, I do know exactly what I'm looking for."

"If everything works out and your bid is accepted, will you oversee the development yourself?"

"Yes. The retirement community will be my business. I'll manage it personally."

"When you're ready for a contractor, I'll introduce you to the woman I work for. You can't get any better than Kasey Hollander. Living here's gonna be a big change for you. You're not going to find the excitement you're used to in New York."

"Good."

Some changes in life seem to be so gradual that they go virtually unnoticed over periods of years. Others occur so quickly and dramatically that they're practically unbelievable. The change, about to take place in Sage Bristo's life, hinged considerably closer to the unbelievable end of the spectrum. As long as she had dreamed of finding a place her soul could call home, the swiftness of its actuality still amazed her.

Part II

Two years later

Chapter 15

Deanne let herself in Sharon's front door, a few minutes late tonight. More anxious that usual she hurried downstairs to friendly greetings from the six women she played cards with twice a month. Tonight she would be meeting a new euchre partner; hopefully one with more staying power than the last few substitutes. Her ex had hung in for about a month after their prolonged breakup. But since then, the pickings for fill-in partners had grown thin. A new partner was inevitable. Sharon, bless her heart, and her tremendous social appeal, had not stopped looking.

"Good news, Deanne," Sharon exclaimed, with her usual boisterousness. "Since we've moved to Thursday nights, we've

79

gained my other housemate. She has some hot date every Wednesday," she teased at the tall, imposing woman emerging from the kitchenette. "But, Thursdays, lucky us, she's free. Sage Bristo, this is Deanne Demore. She's the photojournalist I told you about."

Sage offered a pretty smile and her hand, and locked her deep brown gaze into Deanne's. "It's nice to meet you. You shot Kasey and Connie's ceremony last month."

Pleased at not having put off her hair appointment and for choosing her most flattering sweater for tonight, Deanne smiled a dimpled smile. Her green eyes peered brightly beneath wispy strands of honey-gold at the woman before her. She was neatness personified. *Probably irons her jeans and hangs up her T-shirts.* "Yes," she replied. "I've heard a lot about you. It's nice to finally meet you."

A flood of rumored descriptions raced through her mind at the touch of the smooth slender hand: the queen of ecstasy, mistress of seduction, Dr. Feelgood. She'd heard them all, descriptions both abominable and disturbingly exciting. Deanne wondered as she enjoyed the warmth of it how many women had come to that hand. And wondered, at the sight of Sage's sensuously curved lips how many women hungered for their return, had even believed their lies. Or, maybe she'd never had to lie.

Sage removed her hand. "My sister and I used to be unbeatable back home, but, it's been a few years since I've played."

"That's okay. We lucked out tonight. We're playing Sharon and Laura." She smiled. A little dash of sarcasm was all she needed; it would neutralize this annoying nervousness.

"What?" Sharon asked gruffly.

"She gets so distracted by Laura, she doesn't even know who dealt the last hand." Sharon's impudent expression made her laugh, and created a most captivating smile on Sage's face.

"You're so full of shit," protested Sharon.

80

"Admit it. I beat you with a partner who'd never played before."

Sage leaned forward, as if speaking only to Deanne. "That's all right. We'll just let her keep thinking we're the ones with the terrible disadvantage."

"Stop talking like I'm not standing right here, and get ready to have your cute little asses kicked!" Sharon growled.

"She's such a poop sometimes." Sage still spoke defiantly only to Deanne. "And I thought love would smooth those sharp edges."

Deanne smiled and took her seat facing her new partner. "Did she explain the point system?"

"Yes. Tonight's winners and losers play each other next time. We total our points for both nights, and the team with the most points chooses where they want to be taken to dinner."

"That's it. Pretty simple."

"What kind of food do you like?"

Deanne smiled at her confidence. "Almost any kind. I only have to avoid milk products."

"I don't think I'd be picking a restaurant just yet, Sage. You do have to play some cards here." — Sharon raised a cocky eyebrow at her — "and win more points than anyone else. We've taken Kasey and Connie to dinner three months in a row now," she warned. "I'm beginning to think married couples should extend a handicap."

"We won't need a handicap," insisted Sage. Her eyes came back to Deanne's, holding them at will, until she decided to release them.

Deanne couldn't define the feeling it gave. A sense of exclusiveness, perhaps, as if she was the special recipient of some private confidence. She breathed it in, as she breathed air.

"The higher they ride, the harder they fall," chided Sharon, plunking her short heavy frame into her chair. Laura exchanged pleasantries and joined her, easing her round buxom form into the seat facing Sharon.

"You ready over there?" called Sharon, addressing the table where Kasey and Connie prepared to play Ali and Jan.

"I sense an upset in the air," crowed Ali.

Kasey only laughed, "My knees are shaking."

"Let's play," declared Sharon, dealing the first hand.

Deanne and Sage played the first game devoid of strategy and guessing at intent. They accepted the luck of the cards and the resulting eight points. As they played on, Sage's eyes remained transfixed on Deanne's, giving no indication at all of what they were learning. Deanne's eyes, animated and quick, darted between her cards and her opponents and the fascinating woman across from her. Her eyes, she knew, were at times too expressive for cards, as they searched for clues and struggled for decisions. Still, Sage's stoic expressionlessness more than compensated, and they won the second game easily.

Ahead on points in the third, Deanne found herself relaxing noticeably and enjoying a study of her partner. Sage's long slender fingers, with their impeccably manicured nails, deftly shuffled the cards. They gracefully bent the deck halves into an arch, and collapsed them neatly together. They worked so precisely, so efficiently. She liked how they quickly and smoothly arranged the order of her cards. And she liked the decisive snap they gave to a significant card. Watching Sage's hands was a welcomed relief from Sage's stare and the impossible task of guessing the thoughts behind it. Deanne played her card and continued her study. Sage's finely sculptured left wrist was adorned with four bracelets, two shinning silver, one black rope, and one colorful braid — gifts from past lovers, Deanne speculated, worn like trophies of adoration.

Deanne's reprieve, however, was short-lived. Sage's piercing brown eyes caught her quick glance, daring her to look even deeper. Deanne tried to refocus on the game but had to check twice to remember the lead card. Her concentration was spotty at best, waning often as she watched her partner play. At times, she felt powerless to pull her eyes from the long fingers as they caressed the cards. Later, she caught herself following the long line of her arm across the broad shoulder to where her crisp, upright collar met her well-defined neck muscle. Deanne's fascination continued, down the open 'V' to a small silver figure lying against her chest, until Sage's knowing eyes caught her. Deanne stopped in amazement at their sudden transformation from rigid austerity to liquid warmth; they sparkled like moonlight on rippling water.

"Go out with me," Sage said without warning.

They were in the middle of a hand. Deanne was obviously stunned. "What?"

"Go out with me," she repeated.

"Jesus, Sage," pleaded Sharon. "Give it a rest."

Deanne's eyes darted quickly from Sharon back to Sage. "I don't think that would be a good idea."

"Why not?" Sage asked, with a tone as insistent as her stare.

Deanne's nervousness and sarcasm returned. "And what night would that be?" She hadn't forgotten Sage's Wednesday-night dates and horrendous weekend reputation.

"Choose a night." Sage played her card blindly, her eyes refusing to leave Deanne's.

"Wednesday," she challenged. She couldn't believe she'd uttered it; there was no intention of honoring it.

"Not Wednesday."

Deanne kept her eyes on Sage's. "Then not at all." She smiled, relieved that she was off the hook, more or less.

"Rejected!" exclaimed Sharon with almost sadistic amusement. "I love it!"

The corners of Sage's mouth lifted ever so slightly. "Not a first. Anyone for a drink?" She sent one last glance back at Deanne, then rose and headed for the kitchen.

Still chuckling aloud, Sharon shuffled for the next game.

Sage's honesty about rejection hadn't gone unnoticed. Deanne, like practically everyone else in the gay community knew the story of Sage and Kasey. Only two years ago Kasey had turned down the hot new arrival from New York and dared to say no to the perfection of androgyny who had dated models and a Broadway actress. And, the topper? She'd turned her down because she was in love with a straight woman. The talk hadn't died down until just last month, when Kasey openly married the beautiful Connie Bradford. It was there that Deanne had first seen the infamous Sage Bristo.

Deanne looked at the couple quietly talking at their table. Kasey, an athletic Adonis even at thirty-eight, was as feminine as she was strong. Her singing voice was a divine gift that sent chills through Deanne each time she heard it. And Connie, a dark-haired beauty, strong-willed and feminine, shared her lover's interest in music as well as a need for a lifelong commitment. They were perfect together; they were soul mates. Deanne was glad they had found each other, and glad Kasey had been too smart to fall for the likes of Sage Bristo. Yet for the great seductress to have been told no, in the heat of passion if the story was to be believed, must have been an embarrassing blow, no matter how well she disguised it. For her to be indignant was understandable. However, to develop the friendship she had, with both Kasey and Connie, was a surprise to everyone.

After tonight's introduction to the allure of Ms. Bristo, Deanne had an even greater appreciation for what Kasey must have dealt with. There was a strange flattery attached to just having been asked out. Although she, unlike Kasey, knew the reputation, knew that the interest Sage showed would be fleeting at best, she felt flattered nonetheless.

"Okay, break's over," Sharon called. "Where's Sage?"

"In the kitchen," Connie answered from the other table.

Not yet seated, Deanne offered, "I'll get her."

She swung open the kitchen door thinking about how she might have felt on the other end of her own challenge to Sage and was totally unprepared for what she walked in on. There, wrapped in Sage's arms, was Ali laying claim to a boldly lustful kiss. Murmurs of desire drifted to the doorway, as a tightly clad Ali moved with obvious pleasure. Instantaneously, a flood of embarrassment replaced her earlier feelings of flattery as well as the twinge of guilt for her rudeness. She chided herself for having allowed it. *This* was what she should have expected.

She made concentrated effort to keep her tone matter-of-fact. "Excuse me," she said. "We're ready to start the next game."

"Mmm," groaned Ali. "Has she no consideration?"

Deanne watched Sage ease comfortably into her seat and fought the irritation she felt. To think that she had considered going out with this woman, for even a fraction of second, was frightening. She was too old and too conservative for such nonsense. Flattery was for the naive, one-night stands for those half her age. She wouldn't need a stab in the heart to keep her remindful.

Exactly how they won the last game, Deanne couldn't say. The cards must have fallen correctly; Sage must have played well. Her own ability to concentrate had vanished. It had been replaced with an uneasy disorientation. Her mind, it seemed, was too busy trying to excuse the unexplainable and irrational attraction she felt for this disturbing woman.

"I called the pizza order in. Who's going?" asked Sharon.

"I'll go," offered Sage.

Ali quickly appeared behind Sage's chair. She leaned around her, long dark hair cascading forward, and reached for the half-empty glass. With an overtly intentional move, she brushed her breasts against Sage's cheek.

"Jesus, Ali! Could you be any more obvious?" Sharon snapped.

"If it bothers you, don't look," Ali grinned, seductively sipping from Sage's glass.

Sage's eyes, however, ignored the temptress. They lingered boldly over Deanne's breasts, drifted easily across her shoulders, up her neck, and touched lightly upon her lips before meeting her eyes. That Deanne's eyes followed them the whole time, only seemed to increase Sage's pleasure. She smiled only with the corners of her mouth. A determined Ali leaned to whisper in her ear, deliberately slipping her hand down across Sage's chest.

"Jesus!" exclaimed Sharon, rolling her eyes as she left the table.

Ali straightened. "We're out of beer. I'll go with you."

As the two women disappeared up the stairs, Jan stood and stretched her thin frame. "So much for the novel notion of warm pizza and cold beer. How could you let those two go?"

"Excuse me," Sharon taunted. "I didn't know you wanted to watch."

"As long as we're on the subject," began Deanne, "is there a reason why I'm paired with Don Juanita, instead of Ali?"

Sharon laughed, along with the others. "Well, yeah. We're supposed to be playing cards."

"Deanne," Kasey said as they started for the stairs. There was a remnant of a smile on her face. "This may not seem feasible at the moment, but try to reserve judgment of Sage until you know her better. What you see isn't necessarily what you get."

Deanne respected her longtime friend, but what Kasey asked wasn't going to be easy.

"How else can you take it?" injected Jan. "I don't recall ever seeing her with the same woman more than twice. What's the count now, Sharon?"

"Oh, no. She lives here, remember. I'm sworn to secrecy."

"Okay, never mind," Jan teased. "Everyone knows the bedroom with the revolving door isn't yours."

An obscene gesture from Sharon warranted a scolding from Laura, and the women laughed. The laughter was such an important reason Deanne valued these nights and these women. They had become a vital part of her healing process. While her personal life deteriorated month by month, these women had remained a constant source of encouragement and positive energy. It was the one place, twice a month, where Angie's negativism became neutralized, where the lack of support for her goals and ideas had no effect. In their presence, they allowed only teasing; no verbal abuse was tolerated. The line was very clear. Her feelings were important, her talents appreciated, and her opinions valued. These women were probably more important to Deanne than they would ever realize.

A respectable, albeit not short, time later, Sage and Ali returned with what proved to be warm pizza and cold beer. Sage placed a bag on the table next to Deanne. "You can't have cheese, right?"

"Oh, I forgot to remind Sharon."

"I didn't. I got you a roast beef sub. Is that okay?"

"Yes, thank you."

Sage finally smiled, the full pretty smile that had greeted Deanne at the beginning of the evening. It captivated her again, just as it had then, thoroughly disarming any reason not to smile back. She couldn't remember, at that moment, what had irritated her so. She smiled carefully.

"Well, there was no upset at our table," smiled Connie, hugging Kasey's shoulders and giving her a congratulatory kiss on the cheek. "What happened over there?"

"We took them by eight points," grinned Deanne.

"So did we," exclaimed Kasey.

"Looks like it's a double date for week after next," Sage added.

"It looks like that's the only way you're going to get one," teased Sharon, ruffling the too-perfect hair as she passed Sage's chair.

"Maybe," she said, finding Deanne's eyes.

Chapter 16

"You and Jodie have been seeing a lot of each other lately," Connie remarked during the break. "Anything happening there?"

Deanne smiled at Connie's cut-to-the-chase manner. She never played guessing games. If she wanted to know something, she asked. Kasey had left the table for a refill, but Sage remained, making Deanne think consciously about her answer. "We're just good friends," she said, aware of a slight irritation at herself for not being more spontaneous. She had guarded her answers for too many years; she wasn't going to do it anymore.

"By whose definition?" Connie prodded.

"We both like it the way it is." Deanne's eyes sought out

Sage's reaction, despite her attempt to keep them on Connie. No response registered in the cool brown. "It's nice having a single friend to do things with. We put no demands on each other for anything more than friendship. I like the simplicity of it." More than that, she liked the space that was hers now. She liked the ease with which she could move in and out of her day, writing when she was most productive, setting her schedule so that she could work out. No arguments, no one-sided compromises, no guilt. It was nice.

"Are we ready?" asked Kasey, reclaiming her seat. "They're neck and neck at the other table, too."

"Ready," Sage replied.

At the end of two nights of competition, Deanne was now beginning to recognize certain characteristics in her partner. Sage's knowledge of the game was unmistakable. Her decisions were quick and accurate. Losing didn't rattle her; rather it seemed to quicken her determination. And she took risks, calculated and usually necessary ones. Playing with her was more than enjoyable. It was exciting.

They were tied in the final game at six apiece, but Kasey and Connie led in total points on the night by three. Even if she and Sage picked away, one point at a time, and won the game, they were giving their opponents four chances to win the one point they needed. There was only one other strategy available. One of them had to try a loner, for a quick four-point win. As she evaluated her hand, Deanne marveled at how quickly she had weighed the two risks and assessed a loner as the safer of the two. She doubted she would have seen it the same way a month ago. Looking at her anemic hand, with its lone face card and no aces, she could only hope Sage would use her chance to call if she got it.

Connie turned the ten of diamonds facedown, giving Sage her chance. She looked at Deanne. Despite Deanne's inability to decipher the state of Sage's hand, she suspected her partner was reading her quite well. "Hearts, alone," she said, matter-of-factly. Deanne closed her eyes in relief.

"Ooh, do or die," exclaimed Kasey.

"You're on," Connie added.

The jack of hearts, the obvious lead, sucked out the second bower from Kasey. The ace of clubs forced both Kasey and Connie to follow suit, resulting in two fast tricks, and allowing Deanne to exhale. There didn't seem much cause for concern when Sage's king of hearts fell to the ace she had hoped was buried, since it also flushed the ten of hearts from Kasey's hand. They still had two chances left. Deanne's heart quickened some as Sage snapped down the queen of diamonds. It met Connie's smile and the queen of hearts sliding neatly over it. Deanne automatically held her breath and looked into her partner's eyes. There was a glimpse of something in the brown eyes, but it was undefinable. It all came down to this, as Sage snapped the edge of her last card decisively onto the table. Deanne stared in disbelief at what she knew was the last remaining trump card, the lowly nine of hearts.

"Shit!" yelled Kasey, tossing a black blur across the table and watching Connie's ace of spades fall in defeat. "I don't believe you!" she directed at Sage.

"Yeah!" shouted an excited Deanne, thrusting her hand high over the table.

Sage met her hand, with little more than an inkling of excitement in her face. "I'll bet they're taking us to dinner."

"All right, all right," grumbled Sharon from the other table. "No one here has the points to beat you. I can't believe the first time you two pair up we're taking you to dinner. And beating those two to do it."

"On a do-or-die loner, no less." Connie shook her head in amazement and extended her hand to Sage.

Sharon hovered over the table. "A loner? A little dramatic, wouldn't you say?"

The excitement still glowed on Deanne's face. "It was our only chance. Taking four straight points from these two would have been fantasy."

Sage raised her hand with a smile, and Deanne clasped it.

With a tilt of her head, Sage looked at Sharon. "You put us together."

"Yeah, yeah. Where am I making reservations?"

"Deanne's choice."

Chapter 17

Why was it that she always found herself across the table from this woman? Sage's eyes bored into Deanne's, taking their liberties with her body, recording her reactions. For a while, it seemed logical to Deanne that if she kept eye contact at a minimum, she could avoid the uncontrolled warmth that it always created. However, her strategy proved hopelessly futile. Sage's eyes, met even once, flooded her senses and flushed her skin. She hadn't felt such uncomfortable pleasure since she was too young to know what to do with the advances of Jena Parrish. Jena, with her sinfully good looks and popularity exciting her with her athletic skills and her unexpected pursuit. But age was a factor that couldn't be overcome. And now, as life's irony would have it, she was too old for the advances of Sage Bristo.

"Damn, Deanne. Do you think you could've found a place with more forks?" Sharon frowned as she grumbled, and looked to Sage for her next etiquette cue.

"When was the last time I was taken to dinner?"

"I don't remember."

"Exactly. Do you blame me for taking advantage of this?"

"No, no." Sharon placed a hand on Sage's shoulder and smiled. "As long as Martha here can get me through dinner without embarrassing you all too much."

While the eight women laughed and enjoyed themselves around the long table, the hostess directed a well-dressed man and woman to a table next to them.

"Isn't there another table?" The man asked.

"You reserved a table for two in nonsmoking," she returned. "Is there something wrong with the table?"

"Yes. I don't like the location."

"Chris, they're full," his date explained. "This is fine."

"Next to a table of dykes?"

Seating herself, the woman replied, "It's Friday night. I'm not waiting an hour somewhere else."

Jan and Ali quickly relayed the conversation they heard around the table. The women ate in silence for the next few minutes, enduring the couple's stares, able to hear only bits and pieces of their comments. It was enough, however, to know they were still the main topic. It was too much for Sharon.

"Jan," her voice carried to the end of the table. "Is the orgy at my house or yours tonight?"

"Yours. I'm bringing two new recruits, too."

"Great! That's gonna put you ahead for this month's award."

Quiet laughter traveled the table, with the exception of Laura, who directed a look of censure at the mischievous expression on Sharon's face. "That's enough," she warned.

"What," Sharon replied with the voice of a spoiled child. "Can't I tease the straight people? I promise not to feed them."

It took concentrated effort for Deanne to contain her laughter to a respectable chuckle. The others weren't so successful. Even Sage laughed quietly, while the couple stared at them in defiance. Then Sage neatly folded her napkin and placed it next to her plate. "Excuse me for a minute," she said as she rose.

She moved with the smooth confidence that so intrigued Deanne toward the couple's table. By the time she reached them, she had everyone's attention. She offered a polite nod and smile to the man, who looked as if the president had just appeared in his living room while he was dissing the First Lady. She directed her full attention to the woman.

Ali and Jan, closest to the encounter, strained to hear what Sage was saying. With her back to them, though, it was impossible to discern anything. Whatever it was, it was brief. She walked away, leaving two stunned expressions gaping after her. Then the fireworks began.

"What the hell is she talking about?" he demanded.

"Keep your voice down. I don't know."

"Like you don't know anything about the mysterious flowers that were delivered yesterday?"

"This is crazy. You're calling me a liar, and I've never seen that woman before."

"Yeah well, it sure sounds like she's seen you!"

His face was flushed now; hers beginning to show evidence of anger this confrontation merely brought to a boiling point. "I told you I don't know her," she said, standing abruptly and throwing her napkin to the middle of the table. "But maybe I should." She whirled about sharply and marched toward the door. Outraged, he followed.

With varying degrees of success at curtailing their reactions, the women watched their angry retreat and applauded their departure. Nonchalantly, Sage sipped her drink, nary a hint of expression on her face, until all eyes were once again on her. Her eyes widened in an attempt at innocence as she looked from one to the next. With a questioning look of her own, she shrugged her shoulders.

"Oh, no way," Kasey exclaimed. "You're not leaving this table till we get the dirt."

"Give it up," demanded Sharon.

Sage leaned forward on her elbows, the cocktail glass held gracefully by the fingers of both hands. "All I did was thank her for the dance last week and expressed a wish that we do it again sometime." The only sign of a smile was in her eyes. The rest of the women burst into laughter.

When the fun died to giggles, Connie added, "You realize, of course" — she scanned the faces — "we don't even know what we're laughing at. I'm not ruling out the possibility that Sage did dance with her. But, it's funny either way."

"So, did you?" asked Jan.

Sage looked at the faces, eager for her answer. "When you find you need to know so much about mine, it's time to worry about your own social life."

Sage walked her to her car, where Deanne extended her hand. "Thanks partner, for a wonderful dinner."

"Thank you, for bringing an excitement to the game of euchre I hadn't expected."

Deanne liked the feel of Sage's hand firmly enveloping hers. She left it there longer than usual, enjoying its strength and warmth. "I've been guessing my way along so far. I can't read you yet." She drew back her hand because she knew she should. "But I suspect you play cards like you live."

"And, how is that?"

"Fearless. Willing to take risks. Unafraid of failure. I admire your confidence, your tenacity."

96

"I like your eyes." She tilted her head slightly, looking directly into the eyes considerably more blue today, against the sky. "Along with a lot of other things. And I'm willing to bet there's a change in the way *you're* playing cards these days."

Deanne quickly broke eye contact and pulled her keys from her pocket. "I'd better get going."

"Wait, Deanne. I'd like to apologize for putting you on the spot that first night. I realize it embarrassed you. I should have asked you out, like I am now, privately."

Deanne opened the car door before looking again at the woman who both intrigued and unnerved her. "I appreciate your apology," she said softly. "But, I really think we should leave it at euchre partners."

"I don't bite, at least not on the first date."

"Shall I believe what I've heard about the second?"

"Which is?"

"That everything that's going to happen, happens then, and that the morning after, life goes on."

"Convince me differently."

Deanne smiled and shook her head. "Assuming that's even possible, I don't have the time, or the energy to even attempt it."

"I don't give up easily."

"If you knew anything about me, Sage, you'd understand that we come from vastly different worlds. I could never compete with the kind of women you date. They're young, sexy, uninhibited. I'm . . . not."

"What you've seen, or heard about, are women who are attracted to me. That doesn't always mean the attraction is mutual. Maybe if we got to know each other better, we'd find we're looking for the same things in life."

Deanne slipped neatly into the driver's seat of her car and looked up once more. "Sage, I want to say this as nicely as I can. I will not put myself in a position to be an experiment for you. You'll have to test your relationship skills on someone else. It's too late in my life for me."

The door closed without a good-bye, leaving Sage standing alone in the parking lot.

Chapter 18

A stack of books cradled in one arm and briefcase under the other, Deanne fumbled with the keys to her apartment door. "Shit," she said aloud as they dropped into the freshly fallen snow below. She knelt, carefully balancing her load, and blindly fished out the cold, wet keys. She fumbled again until the key finally slid into the lock and the door swung open.

Two steps into the cramped apartment, the pile of books began to slide. Guiding them in the direction of the couch, she let them go and collapsed alongside the disheveled pile. Exhaustion, the kind where a single breath leaves you teetering on the edge of consciousness, was setting in early. It was only 1:00 in the afternoon. She had only been managing four of her required seven hours of sleep for too many nights now. It was beginning to take its toll.

She closed her eyes. Just for a minute, she promised herself. But the list continued to scroll across the computer screen that used to be her mind. There was one more interview session before the outline on women's prison reform could be firmed. Pictures had to be taken. Two books had to be read by Saturday, for the piece on menopause. The wedding portraits would start at 1:00 Saturday, and the reception was slated to be a long one. That left Sunday to write in order to meet Monday's deadline. It had been this way for over two weeks now, with only a minimal break in sight. But to turn down an assignment or a job meant deciding which bill not to pay. She'd have to find the energy somewhere.

She sighed, and felt her body relax into the soft pillows of the couch. Jackie Madouse, one of her favorite creations, jumped to life. "Workin' at Kroger's ain't no disgrace. Not a lot of spendin' cash. But at 5:00, I got nothin' else on my mind but my woman. I figure, you do this life once; you damn well better do what makes you happy. You sure ain't gonna get a second shot at it." Point well made, girlfriend Deanne smiled.

What would she be willing to give for untethered time to write her books? To give Jackie a suitable venue to offer her boldly honest, albeit simplistic view of the world? Certainly not her freedom again, not at the price she'd paid over the past six years. Never again would she trade her needs for someone else's, or compromise happiness to ease financial burdens. Living with someone who disrespected her six out of seven days because of the hope she received on the seventh was pure insanity. Admitting defeat at saving a relationship was by far healthier than trying to make the impossible work. She had come to realize that respect had more to do with personal integrity than it did with the state of her relationship. Nothing in her power could have made her relationship with Angie a happy one. She had exhausted herself trying. Lost herself, actually. To no avail. She couldn't do it, and she knew that now.

Maybe Angie could be happy living with someone like Jackie Madouse, a woman with no particular designs on leaving her mark on a society she viewed with such irreverence. Angie needed a woman with a regular job and simple needs, with the same social mores and ample time for domestic tasks. Someone who saw the importance of Monday night football and knew who had wild card status. That woman had not been Deanne for a long time. The days were gone when she could tolerate wasted time at softball parties, engrossed in hours of inebriated conversations. Along with those days had gone the tolerance for any complaint not attached to an agenda for change. How many complaints would it take before Jackie would tell her, "All that bitchin's never gonna do what layin' a hot one on your girlfriend's lips, right in the middle of McDonald's, will". Not exactly a Deanne Demore plan of action, but at least she'd be off her tuchas and doing something. No. On second thought, Jackie wouldn't last past the first argument with Angie. How many times would Jackie take being bitched out for leaving a light on or not having the laundry done before she told her where anal tendencies should be retained?

The phone woke her suddenly. Deanne jerked into consciousness with a painful stiffness in her neck. Simultaneously, she grabbed the phone and looked at her watch. Fifteen minutes would probably qualify as a catnap.

"Mom? Mom, calm down. I can't understand you. Is he okay? Did he fall? . . . Okay . . . Okay. No, don't keep trying to lift him . . . No, you're going to hurt yourself. Try to make him as comfortable as you can. Mom . . . Mom, I know . . . Everything's going to be okay. Let me make some phone calls, and I'll be right there. He'll be all right . . . About an hour. Try to reassure him. I love you."

Quickly, she dialed Sage's beeper and began rearranging her schedule one more time. She grabbed an interview tape and stuck it in her briefcase. No sense wasting the forty minutes drive time; she could review it on the way and speak her notes into her little recorder, a procedure that had saved her on many occasions. Before she had time to even make her way to the bathroom, the phone rang. Sage, predictably prompt. She grinned appreciatively.

"I called to let you know I can't play tonight . . . No, I have a family emergency. But my schedule is worse than last week, so I probably wouldn't have made it anyway. No, thanks for offering, though. It's Dad's arthritis. He didn't want to get out of bed today. Mom finally coaxed him up, but he slipped to the floor, and she can't move him . . . Yes, exactly . . . Loss of independence. Anyway, I'll go see if I can get his spirits back up . . . I'm sure. Thanks . . . Probably next week . . . I'm sure you'll live." She laughed easily. "Would you make explanation for me? Thanks. See you next week."

Next week. What would that make it — twelve days? Twelve days without having to look into those magnetic eyes, without having to measure her own reactions or censure uninvited feelings. It should be a welcome relief. Hadn't it been so far?

A few more phone calls and she had things adequately rearranged. There were arguments to be made for working a nine-to-five; someone else's schedule, someone else's headache. Independence, however, whatever its form, whatever its cost, should be cherished. That she believed from the bottom of her soul. She took a deep breath and headed for the bathroom.

* * * * *

102

The knock at her door surprised her; she wasn't expecting anyone. She hurriedly gathered her things. If she was on her way out, certainly no one could expect her to stand and talk long. She opened the door to meet the alluring eyes that dashed her twelve days of freedom.

"Oh, god!" Deanne exclaimed in surprise.

"I wouldn't go that far," Sage said with a smile. "I've never been able to master the miracle thing." Deanne smiled in return, despite the annoying warmth the sight of Sage was creating. "You sounded so tired, I thought maybe you could use some help."

"I'm fine. Really. I'm sure it's nothing I can't handle. You've got a business to run." Deanne started down the walk, undecided as to what exactly to do at this point.

"They can beep me. Besides I brought something I think might help."

Suddenly, ancient concerns, selfish at their very core, overtook her. Deanne found herself worrying about what a woman of New York sophistication and wealth would think of her meager, but humble, upbringing. The adult pride she held for her parents and their struggle to raise five children on a cabinetmaker's salary, fought back and reemerged. Sage Bristo should have something as worthy of her pride, she decided. She caught sight of a wheel visible in the back of the black Explorer. "He said he'd kill himself rather than live out his life in a wheelchair."

"It's not a wheelchair. It's a streamlined version of those motorized carts you see in the big department stores. Small enough to go through regular doorways." She opened the back to give Deanne a better look. "He doesn't have to use it all the time, only when he needs it."

"Would I be renting it from you?"

"Let's see if he likes it first. Hop in and tell me where we're going."

"Hang a louie at the light." Deanne saw the edge of a grin on Sage's face. "Sorry, I didn't mean to regress that far.

Whenever I come back here, it brings back a lot of childhood feelings."

"And what was childhood like for the cutest little dyke in Michigan?"

"It's another three miles after the road turns to dirt."

"You're more comfortable with the word *lesbian*, aren't you?"

"I am, but that's not why I hesitate to answer." Deanne's eyes met Sage's straight on. "We come from completely different worlds. I want to remind you of that before we get there."

"You've got three miles to tell me all you can."

"Pretty boring stuff."

"If it gets too bad I'll signal you with a big yawn."

Deanne smiled. *Could it really be this easy?* "You asked for it. Oldest of five children. Raised in a family rich in love, and dirt-poor in material wealth. Each of Jon and Eleanor's children learned that what made you worthy of God's bounty was honesty and hard work. We learned early that mistakes were merely building blocks and that honesty spared us the rod."

"I'm riveted. But I crave details." Houses built like little boxes began to appear more frequently along the rural road. They told part of the story more clearly than words. Poverty, or very close, was evident by worn-out cars, plastic taped over broken windows, and children's toys scattered in unkempt yards.

"We ate out of our garden in the summer and canned for the winter. Until I was in the third grade, we had a hand pump at the kitchen sink, and no hot water. We used an outhouse during the day, and slop buckets at night. But our house was always in good repair, and we were all neat and clean and loved. Mom cleaned other peoples' houses while we were in school." Deanne met Sage's eyes momentarily. "It's the gray house with the big willow tree."

"And not a single yawn."

* * * * *

An anxious Eleanor Demore, dressed in the pink-and-mint-green sweatsuit Deanne had given her, met them at the door. "It worried me so; I hid his gun in the shed," she whispered before leading them into the tiny bedroom. There, pillows cushioning his back and head against the side of the bed, was an obviously disabled Jon Demore. He looked up at them from his awkward position on the floor and shook his head.

Deanne knelt and took the gnarled hand in hers. She talked quietly with him before she stood again. She addressed Sage in the doorway. "He's embarrassed for you to see him like this."

"I don't see that we have another choice. You can't lift him alone." Sage stepped over his legs and positioned herself on his right side as Jon watched her silently. Her words were spoken as she knelt and looked into his eyes. "Deanne and I are going to give you a shoulder up here, and when you're on your feet, we'll have a proper introduction, face-to-face." He nodded his resignation and lifted his arm to her shoulders.

"Dad, we're going to do this in two stages. To the edge of the bed first, then to your feet. Okay? On three, Sage."

Together they lifted, maneuvering his weight, unassisted by stiffened joints, to the bed. When he did stand, painfully and with one hand still grasping Deanne's shoulder, Sage moved away and faced him. "Mr. Demore, I'm Sage Bristo," she said, extending her hand in greeting.

The thick fingers gripped firmly. With more dignity than was ordinarily possible in flannel pajamas, he squared his shoulders. "How do you do."

"We'll get out of here, Dad, so you can get dressed. We need to get some things from the car. Let us know if you need any help, Mom."

"Will you stay for dinner and visit?"

Sage nodded to Deanne.

"Sure, Mom."

Jon Demore emerged from the hallway, labored steps showing their pain on his weary face. He was met by the whir of the battery-powered cart Deanne maneuvered around the sofa.

"No, Deanne," he said firmly, refusing his wife's assistance to be seated in his chair. "When I can no longer walk, it's time for me to go."

"Don't talk like that, Dad. You're too important to us."

"I'm no good to anyone this way." His eyes were distant, tired. His brow furrowed, forming deep lines between them.

Deanne sat on the arm of his chair, wrapped her arms around his shoulders, and kissed the side of his head. "And who would I trust my stories to? Who would be as honest? Who would tell me of the days long ago that might go forgotten?" He patted her arm affectionately. "Nope," she said, kissing his head again. "You can't go anywhere. I've got too much to learn. Will you entertain Sage for me, while I help Mom with dinner?"

"I'll do my Sunday-school best."

Sage, meanwhile, had entertained herself examining the pictures housed in old rectangles and squares that covered the wall behind the couch. Three girls, stepping-stones, always in order. Two little boys, scrubbed and grinning. Parents beaming and proud, growing older and grayer as their children, one after the other, grew and graduated. Marriages and new families. Sage returned to the laughing little girl over the lamp. Telltale dimples identified her as Deanne — four years old, maybe five, holding up oversized pants, cuffed many times, shirt to her knees, and laughing so hard you could almost hear her.

"My little Dee Berry," Jon said from his chair behind her. "Our firstborn treasure."

"She was a happy little girl."

"Sensitive, but easy to please. Little Dee Berry. I haven't heard her laugh like that for such a long time."

Sage looked again at the picture. Was there ever a time in her own life when she felt that much joy?

"She's a writer, you know."

Sage nodded.

"A good writer. She can touch your heart with her words, make it sing or make it cry."

"I follow her articles. She is good."

He shook his head and motioned with his hand. "Below there, below the lamp. Open the door, there's a box." Sage retrieved the worn old box and brought it to him. Stiffened fingers carefully lifted one of the folders and handed it to her. "Her stories. You have to read her stories."

"Do you want me to read it now?"

"Yes, read that one; there's time before dinner."

She settled on the worn-out couch a few feet away and began to read. Page after page moved her deeper into the web of emotions that bound the hearts and minds of the characters that were so real she could see their faces. She was unaware of the sounds from the kitchen or the ongoing conversation between the other three people in the little house. The people on the pages had taken her with them, transported her to a world she knew little about. Before she realized it, she was reading out of need, the need to know more about them, to know they would be all right. And hidden deep in that need was a need to know more about Deanne Demore. She didn't hear Eleanor's first call to dinner.

"Come on, you two." Eleanor repeated from the doorway. "Oh, you have her reading, Jon."

Her voice pulled Sage from the pages. "I'm sorry," she said. "I got lost in this story. I've only one page to go."

"I keep waiting for her to write new ones. I've read those over and over." Eleanore swept her hand before the wall of pictures. "The others have their children, Deanne has her stories. I know them now like my grandchildren. Come along when you're through." She and Sage helped Jon to his feet, and Sage finished the last page standing.

They linked hands around the table as warm delicious smells of a home-cooked meal filled the small kitchen and Jon Demore offered his prayer of thanks. Sage bowed her head reverently, but her mind continued its appreciation of the talents of the woman whose hand she held. *Her words are her children. Yes, Eleanor was right. They fulfilled her need to create; they passed on her experiences, her thoughts, her legacy. It made perfect sense.* Affectionately, she rubbed her thumb over Deanne's fingers, then squeezed her hand gently again at the amen.

"What do you do, Sage?" Jon asked while his wife filled his plate.

"I run a retirement community called Longhouse on the Lake."

"I've seen the advertisement on television," acknowledged Eleanor. "Oh, and it looks so beautiful, with the lake and the gardens."

"Thank you. I fell in love with the land the minute I saw it. You know, many of those are the residents' own gardens. They're very proud of them. They love to show them off whenever I bring people through." Sage looked over at Deanne. "Why don't you bring your folks one day for lunch, and I'll give you the winter tour. We have some beautiful inside gardens," she directed at Eleanor.

"Oh, let's do, Deanne." Her mother's eyes twinkled with excitement that was hard to refuse.

"Deanne, take your mother. She's stuck here with me most all the time now."

"There are some things I'd like you to see, too, Mr. Demore. And, something I'd like to talk with you about."

"I'd never be able to walk far enough to see much of anything."

Sage looked at him and smiled. "That's why we have those motorized carts. And there's no snow or ice to worry about. The sidewalks and driveways are specially heated from below." She redirected her eyes to Deanne, who seemed unusually quiet. "These days golfers don't even walk the distance anymore."

"The three of us will go, Dad, okay?"

"I'm serious about your Dad teaching in our Learn from the Masters Program." The Explorer came to a halt on the uneven accumulation of ice and snow in front of Deanne's apartment. "He may not be able to work the wood like he used to, but he can teach others how. He's the master of a dying craft. Who better to pass it down?"

"Sage, I know you were trying to make him feel better, but it's not fair to get their hopes up about something like that. As much as I would love to have them live in that kind of beauty and luxury before they die, there's no way we can afford for them to live at Longhouse. Even if they could get thirty for the house, it just isn't possible."

"But it is possible. Besides individual homes, there are apartments right in the Longhouse itself. The residents' bills are paid by the interest from the money they've invested. The capital belongs to their family and is always returned to the family. Plus, there are grants available, and your father would be paid well for teaching."

"I don't know, Sage."

"Your mother needs stimulation to feel vital; you can see it in her eyes. And your father needs to feel useful and worthy."

"I know that. But they do not need enormous financial stress."

"And if I could convince you that they wouldn't have?"

"It would take some convincing, I'm afraid."

Sage rested her arm on the back of Deanne's seat and leaned toward her. "I'll work on that later." She leaned closer. Eyes, shining black in the dim light, moved on Deanne's mouth. Soft lips brushed her cheek.

Deanne turned her face away from the sensuous, teasing lips, yet her heart beat like the wings of a captured bird. She turned away from the instant it would take to give herself to this woman.

"Just a kiss," Sage whispered, her hand gently cupping Deanne's flushed face.

"No, Sage. I don't like what I'm thinking right now."

Sage retreated slowly to her side of the car. "I'll bet I won't either."

Deanne looked directly at her. "For the sake of even a friendship." — her eyes narrowed and darkened — "you'd better not be using those two people to get to me."

Sage stiffened. The eyes that had sent such warmth through Deanne now sent a wave so chilling it made her shiver. "I don't think anyone has ever so directly insulted my integrity." The large jaw muscle flexed into a darkened edge. "For now, I'm going to attribute it to your distorted and ill-advised opinion of my character and hope that later you can be more objective."

"You're making it hard for me to be objective."

"No, you're making it hard, with your unquestioning acceptance of rumors and your damn age phobia."

"Deny you've been with more women than you can remember."

"Admit that you don't really know me."

110

"You're right, I don't." She snatched the tape from the dash, and swung open the door. "And I don't think I want to."

The door slammed shut with a blast of chilled air, and Deanne's darkened figure disappeared into the shadows of the building.

Chapter 18

"I never expected you to come and get me." Deanne slipped into the front seat of the Explorer and brushed the snow from her hair.

"Did you expect me to play loner hands all night?" Sage asked with a grin.

"No. After my little tantrum last week, I expected you to send someone else." She held up her hand. "I know. That only proves how little I know about you."

Sage responded with only a smile.

"It's my turn to apologize. I haven't given you the benefit of the doubt. I'm sorry."

"Accepted."

"I promise to try harder not to make assumptions . . . if you promise to humor my age phobia."

There was an unusual, but quick, frown from Sage. "It's so senseless, Deanne. I must be older than you think I am."

"Twenty-nine."

"Please. I'm thirty-one. And, in New York years, I should be checking into a retirement community, not running one."

"I'm forty-three, Sage." She smiled and answered the shocked look on Sage's face. "Yes, forty-three."

Sage stared in apparent disbelief until she had to force her eyes back to the road.

Deanne continued to answer the unasked questions. "I highlight my hair to hide the gray, moisturize religiously every day, drink lots of water, and devote a serious amount of time to working out."

"It works."

Connie emerged from the stairway, a plate of homemade cookies in hand. "Deanne's battery is dead. Sage went to pick her up. She said she'd be back by the time these were done."

"Mmm," Kasey grinned. "Why am I not surprised that she isn't?"

"She'll have her in bed by next week," boasted Sharon, as she helped herself to a napkin and three cookies. "I can't believe it's taking so long, though."

Ali sacrificially passed the plate. "She's not her type."

"I don't think type has anything to do with it," interjected Kasey. "Deanne's not only the most conservative woman I know, she's also the most emotionally sensitive. Sage scares her."

"Maybe," added Connie. "But I still think —-"

"Sorry I held everything up," Deanne apologized, bursting into the room. "I've just been reminded why I hate automobiles."

Sage strode in immediately behind her. "Are our next victims ready?"

"We're waiting for Jan, now," explained Kasey.

"Not anymore," Sharon reported from the other side of the room. "That was her on the phone. She's heavin' chunks. I guess we're destined not to play tonight."

"Now what? And, please, don't anyone say Pictionary," pleaded Ali.

Laura finally joined them, ladened with additional plates of snacks.

"We could all gorge ourselves on fattening snacks and watch Ali drool," Connie teased.

"There's nothing more obnoxious," declared Sharon, "than a woman who can snap her jeans straight out of the dryer."

Laura watched her dear love reach for a handful of Fiddle-Faddle, and couldn't resist. "Look around you, sweetie. You and I are the only ones here who can't do that."

The laughter didn't daunt her. Sharon helped herself to a few more snacks, filling her plate. "I know . . . it's disgusting."

"I'll go get some videos," offered Kasey.

"Wait, here." Sharon grabbed a book from under the table. "Everyone sit down. I've been dying to try this lesbian game book. Let me find something."

The women abandoned their tables for the cozier seating of unmatched chairs and an old sofa that was enjoying a second life in the corner of the basement. Deanne found herself inadvertently sitting next to Sage on the sofa. Initially, she welcomed the break from the relentless gaze and its disturbing warmth. But she soon found that sitting so close that their bodies touched and the smell of her perfume was even more disturbing.

"Here we go," smiled Sharon. "This ought to prove interesting; we have so many unique egos gathered here. It's a list of questions, from 1 to 150. When it's your turn, give me a number, and you have to answer that question. Then you can pick another person to answer the same question."

"This could prove dangerous," Ali advised, settling into the green overstuffed chair and leaning her head back.

"No one said we have to tell the truth," smiled Laura.

"You couldn't lie if your life depended on it," Sharon quipped. "All right. Starting clockwise, that means you, Connie."

"Ninety-five."

"Question ninety-five is . . . yes! Describe your most erotic fantasy."

"Hmm, I've never even heard this," Kasey grinned.

"Yes you have — every time we make love." Kasey's embarrassment only made Connie smile and the others giggle. "Kasey is my fantasy." Connie looked into the eyes of her lover, then leaned over and kissed her.

"Good answer," applauded Laura. "Good answer."

"But boring. Come on, whose fantasy do you want to hear?" Sharon anxiously directed.

Connie looked from face to face. She made her decision more to juice things up a bit than from her own curiosity. "Ali."

Relieved to be spared from this one, Deanne happily directed her curiosity to the sultry Ali.

"I'm lying naked on a deserted beach," she began.

"I'm liking it already," Sharon giggled.

"Suddenly, I'm aware of an incredibly sexy dyke striding up the beach wearing only a pair of loose-fitting cutoffs. She's dark and brooding and says nothing, just straddles me, blocking the sun. The pants are so loose I can pull them down without unfastening them. She steps out of them and drops to her knees over me. I take her in my mouth and bring her to an orgasm that shakes her so hard that she falls to her hands. When she regains her strength, she takes me. Just as

I catch my breath, she takes me again, and again. I'm helpless to stop her. Finally, when I can no longer move, she picks me up and carries me off."

"To live in ecstasy evermore," signed Laura.

"Jesus!" exclaimed Sharon. "What a creamer!"

"What we lack in movie sex, we sure make up for with Ali's fantasies," added Kasey.

"In other words," Deanne mused, "if you're suddenly missing, we shouldn't call the police or form a search party."

"I'm sorry, I don't have Connie's idealism. To me, a fantasy is only a fantasy." Ali characteristically swept her hair to the side and reached for her drink. "There's nobody that good."

"We can all dream, can't we?" added Deanne.

"Kasey, it's your turn. Pick a number," ordered Sharon.

"Ten."

"What decision do you regret most in your life?"

Kasey leaned forward on her thighs and thoughtfully focused on the glass she rolled slowly between her palms. "For more than one reason, not coming out sooner. I'd have been a lot happier sooner in my life." She looked lovingly at Connie. "And I wouldn't have put Connie through hell or hurt anyone else's feelings."

There was a respective silence before Sharon asked, "Whose regret would you like to hear?"

She looked directly at the woman on her left. "Sage."

Sage directed a quick wink and a subtle smile privately to Kasey before she began. "Maybe a better question would be, 'Why regret something that can't be changed?' It seems a terrible waste of time and energy."

Exactly the kind of unemotional response she would expect of her, Deanne thought, watching the unmoved profile beside her.

"If you don't analyze your decisions, how can you learn from your mistakes and make better decisions next time?" asked Laura.

"No two situations are identical. Just the fact that it's the second time a similar situation occurs makes it unique. It requires an independent decision. We all make the best decision we can, with what we know at the time."

"No regrets," summarized Deanne.

She kept her response impersonal by focusing on placing her glass on the table in front of her. "Never."

"Well, that makes me feel better already," declared Sharon. "Why don't you give us a number professor? It's your turn."

"Give me forty-three."

Deanne ignored the implication. Sharon cleared her throat, and grinned as she searched. "Okay. Forty-three wants to know, 'What are the most significant words ever spoken to you by a woman.' " She snickered, along with the others, and quipped 'Your place or mine?' "

Ali added to the chuckles, "I hope you'll have the decency to keep private what I said to you in the heat of passion."

"You're demented lesbians," replied Sage seriously. "I only tolerate your insolence because I'm masochistic by nature. Otherwise, I'd have no use for you at all."

"Are you gonna answer the question or play shrink with us?" chided Sharon.

"If you concentrate real hard on opening your minds, I'll answer the question." She shifted her position, leaning comfortably against the arm of the couch. "I was helping my grandmother sort out boxes of things in her attic. I watched as she carefully lifted an old half-empty pack of cigarettes from a drawer. It wasn't so much what she said but the look in her eyes when she spoke. 'These were in your grandfather's pocket when he died,' she said. 'I don't know why I kept them.' She looked into my eyes when she said, 'They're no good to anyone now, are they?' I saw the tears as they formed in her eyes, and it blew me away. After forty years, she had tears in her eyes." Sage stiffened as she took a deep breath. "Anyone for another drink?" she asked, rising from the couch.

Deanne watched her take drink orders and walk straight and tall to the kitchenette. She looked from face to face around the circle. The expressions varied little; all confirmed Deanne's own unexpressed surprise. Sage Bristo did show emotion. It was deep and well protected, but it was nice to know it was there. She might well become a character in a Demore novel yet.

"Number, Ms. Demore."

"Eighty."

"You're jogging through a park early one morning, when you hear what sounds like a woman in trouble. As you get closer you can see a woman struggling against a man in the bushes beside the path." Deanne leaned her head back against the couch. There was no doubt where this was headed. "Do you: Keep running to the nearest phone at the edge of the park? Get close enough to get a description of the man, then continue to the phone? Or pick up a tree branch lying nearby and try to stop the attack?"

"I had a feeling I'd get one of these," Deanne sighed. "No doubt, there will be disagreement with my answer." She felt Sage's position shift against her shoulder. "I know common sense speaks loudly to going on to a phone, which would leave me hoping that the police would get there quickly. That same common sense would tell me, though, that rape or even murder would happen before help got there. Getting close enough for a description may or may not distract him, but I know I couldn't leave her."

"You'd attack?" asked a surprised Ali.

"I'd be yelling for help the whole time, but, yes, I'd try to stop it."

"I don't know if I can say what I'd do until I was faced with the real thing," Connie remarked.

Sage moved suddenly forward, placing her hand over Deanne's knee. She looked back at her as she rose. In her eyes was a seriousness that seemed to transcend that of the conversation. It was a look that instilled immediate concern. Concern for Sage Bristo; now, there was a contradiction in thought Deanne had never expected.

Sage disappeared up the stairs, and the conversation continued. Weapon or no weapon, you wouldn't have known. Personal safety must be considered above all else. The discussion carried on around her, while Deanne's own thoughts traveled back years. Suddenly, she was running hard again with Nikki, their hearts racing in fear, outrunning the two boys in the alley. Faster than Nikki, she was running ahead of her, listening for Nikki's cues to turn right or left. Barely, she cleared an unexpected ditch, scrambling over the rough mound of dirt and gravel. Then she heard her friend's cry for help. Without thought, with adrenaline shooting through her body, she went back for her. Pulled her from the ditch, right at the feet of their pursuers. Together they had thrown dirt in their faces, and escaped to safety. Together there was always a chance. Alone, she didn't like to think about. No, she could not leave the woman in the bushes.

When Sage finally returned, the women were picking up dishes and preparing to leave. "We can give Deanne a ride home," Kasey offered.

"Thanks, but I'd like to take her home," Sage returned quietly.

"I suspected as much."

Deanne joined the gathering by the stairs. "Kase, are we going with the pyramid, and increasing weight tomorrow?"

"Yeah, let's try it; especially with the quads. I'm going to challenge you on the abs, too."

"You must have been working hard. I'm up to 350 crunches with the weight."

"I know. I'm ready."

Sage politely held Deanne's jacket just behind her left shoulder. "Sage, I can hitch a ride with Kasey."

"That's all right, it's my pleasure," she said, as Deanne slipped into the warm wool.

The group made their way up the stairs, and said their good-byes in the entranceway. Ali, at the front, opened the door into the first rush of cold winter air, then turned back around. "Just a piece of advice," she said, aiming her words at Deanne. "If you're thinking about fucking her, don't waste your time. She's highly overrated."

The shock registered immediately on Deanne's face, while Sharon burst into raucous laughter. Sage, with nary a hint of a smile, merely feigned a pained expression, and coolly replied, "Does this mean I'm out of the running for Lesbian Lover of the Year?"

"I'm afraid so," laughed Kasey.

"I'm devastated," she said, clutching a gloved hand to the front of her jacket, and watching Ali depart with movements as brisk as the winter night.

The Explorer rolled easily through the city street rutted with now frozen slush. Kenny G blew the soulful sounds of *Breathless* around them. Deanne found that the woman who perplexed her so, was much more easily studied in profile. Long lashes shrouded mysteries in the dark eyes beneath them. She almost hated to have the mysteries dispelled. There was a sense of safety in not knowing. Emotions could remain comfortably in limbo. Yet she was compelled to ask. "Did you sleep with Ali?"

The eyes carefully came around. "Does it matter?"

"It does to me."

Her eyes went back to the street. "Why? Will it affect whether or not you sleep with me?"

"No. I base that decision on love."

"Then my answer's irrelevant. Besides, if I say yes, my lovemaking ability is in question. If I say no, it leaves you wondering if I denied it to save face. Either way, you still don't know why she said what she did."

"Or how many other discontented women you've left in your wake."

A sly smile greeted her this time. "Or satisfied? Hundreds, if my reputation is to be believed."

"Is it? I'm not assuming anymore, remember?"

"I don't pretend to be a model of virtue. That reputation didn't appear out of nowhere. But I'm afraid it has become terribly distorted. It precedes me wherever I go and remains in spite of me. I can't seem to live it down, and I'm sure it's humanly impossible to live up to."

"What people see is influenced by what they've heard."

Sage finally returned a warm genuine smile. "It would be nice, just for once, to be seen for who I really am."

"I've honestly been trying."

Sage pulled into the drive and turned her full attention to Deanne. "Would now be a good time to ask you to dinner and a show next Friday?"

"No."

"No, it wouldn't be a good time, or no, I'm declining?"

"No, I'm declining."

"Saturday?"

"No, Sage."

Sage leaned back against her door and draped her arm over the steering wheel. "Okay," she said with a tilt of her head. "I need some pictures taken for a new brochure at Longhouse. Can I hire you?"

"That's your trump card? You're not trying to hide this strategy, are you?"

"I've obviously reached an all-time low."

"I won't be able to do any additional work until after the holidays. As it is, I don't know how I'm going to get everything done."

"My sister's going to spend a week with me after the first of the year. Maybe we can schedule a day while she's here. I'll plan lunch for us."

Deanne smiled at her.

"I really want you to meet Cimmie."

"You play a mean game of cards, Lady."

The laughter they shared was light and easy for the first time since they'd met. It was a nice feeling she had, as Deanne reached for the door.

"Are you going to Sharon's New Year's Eve party?"

"Except for my family get-together, it's the only social event I'm allowing myself. I'll be there . . . with Jodie."

Chapter 19

At the base of the stairs, Deanne handed her slip of paper to Sharon the Pooh, "the cartoon character she was most like". Pooh looked from the paper to Deanne's purple-and-green sweatsuit. "Deanne! What are you supposed to be? You drew 'your secret self.' " A glance at Jodie, standing beside her, offered no clue. Hating the whole idea of a costume, Jodie had only consented to a conservative suit and tie.

"Ice. American gladiator."

"Yeah, Deanne!" shouted Kasey. "Take it off, honey. Give Pooh-bear heart failure."

A various array of famous females and cartoon characters shouted and whistled encouragement. Deanne blushed and laughed. "Let me get in the door, and get comfortable first."

She turned to Jodie as they looked for a place to settle. "Why did I do this?"

"Where's Sage?" Catwoman Connie inquired of Pooh.

"She'll be here, late enough to make a goddamn grand entrance."

"Who's she bringing?"

"I have no idea. I don't even know what she's wearing. She left her slip on the coffee table, so I cheated and looked. She drew 'how others see you.' It ought to be interesting, if nothing else."

Someone noticed Deanne removing her sweatsuit and fists began winding in excitement. The room erupted into a raucous "woo-woo-woo." To their enjoyment, the disrobing revealed a beautifully sculptured body, trim and tight from head to foot, with well-defined muscles shaping her shoulders and legs.

Kasey smiled her approval of her friend's hard work, displayed in a pair of bright red shorts and a stars-and stripes-sports bra. Deanne playfully threw her sweatpants at her. "Quit." She laughed, thoroughly enjoying the attention. It was rare that anyone other than her workout partner had the chance to appreciate the results of her workouts.

"Mm, mm, mm. Femme on the streets, butch in the sheets," quipped Wonder Woman. "Have I overlooked something very interesting?"

"I don't think so, Ali."

Holding up a pair of jousting weapons, Jodie announced, "We will entertain all challengers, after they've had about three drinks."

Suddenly the mood in the room quieted to hushed whispers. Deanne followed the stares of the others, to the bottom of the stairs. The sight there took her breath away.

Sage took the final step into the room, dressed in tight, black-leather pants laced up the front, and a large-sleeved peasant shirt unbuttoned between her breasts. A black velvet cape majestically draped one shoulder. Her eyes were shaded with the wide brim of a black hat; that had one side folded up to secure a white plume. Nothing more needed to enhance the effect. She strode with natural grace into the room, with the carriage of an aristocrat. She was alone.

"Don Juanita," Deanne declared under her breath.

"What?" Jodie asked.

"Nothing."

"Well, shit," exclaimed Sharon. "There goes my hope of dozens of women petting me affectionately and cuddling into my fur."

Laura slapped the thick yellow fur. "Oh, stop it. You're damn lucky you have this woman to pet and cuddle with."

Age notwithstanding, attention from two women certainly goes a long way toward healing a damaged ego, even if one of them was Sage Bristo. Strangely, to be counted among the many felt like a compliment, albeit, not a big one, and not one comparable to the years of Jodie's love and friendship, but a compliment nonetheless. The feelings generated by each were, of course, quite different, as vastly different as the two women themselves. Sweet Jodie, mature and stable, offered proven loyalty and affection; Sage Bristo offered excitement. Deanne couldn't deny that she had never met anyone with a presence so compelling, even with all the events she'd covered and all the interviews. There had not been one other so captivating. Sage merely appeared in the room, and like metal slivers drawn to a magnet, thoughts and reactions suddenly, and helplessly, sought her out. Looks alone couldn't hold that kind of attention, at least not for long. It was more than physical attractiveness. It was the way she carried herself; the proud

hold of her head, the reserved self-assurance of her movements, the complete control over emotion. It was no damn
wonder she had her pick of women, eager, willing young
things, with few inhibitions and fewer demands for commitment. They weren't afraid to make themselves known.

For Deanne, making the choice at age twenty-four
wouldn't have been difficult. Making it now shouldn't be
either. Nevertheless, she had to admit, having two women
vying for her attention, tempted her to enjoy the challenge a
little too much and languish a little too long in the competition. She cautioned herself against it. *Enjoy in moderation,
maintain reasonable perspective.*

Arms draped along the sloping arms of the overstuffed
chair, Sage lounged comfortably, watching Deanne and
Connie's futile attempts at coaxing Jodie to dance. Sharon,
minus her Pooh head now, dropped herself heavily onto the
couch next to her. "Jesus. Did you see those abs?"

"Hadn't noticed."

Sharon contorted a questioning scowl toward her friend,
whose gaze had not left the dancing women. Suddenly, their
collective view was blocked by another midriff, one clad with
Wonder Woman's large gold buckle. Sage moved her gaze up
over the prominent bust line to find Ali's eyes measuring the
gap in material between her breasts. They moved boldly from
one nipple to the other, observing the unrestrained push of
them beneath the soft material. Sage followed her eyes coolly.
"That should be against the law," Ali said finally.

"Why not?" Sage quipped as she rose. "What you have in
mind is." She slid past Ali, as Sharon collapsed in hardy
laughter.

* * * * *

From the beginning of the evening, the situation had been apparent. If Deanne drank quietly with Jodie, Sage watched. If she talked politely with Sage, Jodie watched. Deanne danced with everyone who would, and they both watched. It became easy to let the music be her connective tissue, drawing her from person to person, keeping her body in motion and giving her mind a wonderful feeling of detachment. She danced with this one and that one, without concern that on the way home she would be dealing with unfounded jealousy. She laughed and sang along with the others with less inhibition than she had felt in years. Tonight she didn't have to watch every word as if it would touch off a potential argument, or deal with demands for affection that had long since been destroyed. Tonight she felt respected and loved and even sexy.

Deanne danced happily, smiling at Kasey's suggestive moves with innocent appreciation. She loved Kasey; she probably would have fallen in love with her, had they ever been free to date each other at the same time. But like some things in life, it wasn't meant to be. They openly respected and appreciated each other's talents, which was a special relationship in itself. And they teased as close to the edge of respectability as they could, because it was fun and it felt good. To say that they had never had Angie's trust was a gross understatement, but they'd had Connie's, and that's all that counted now.

Deanne smiled again as Kasey narrowed the distance between them. She was teasing with that come-on look, and Deanne knew it was okay to enjoy it. Then she moved closer yet. Deanne's smile was transformed into a questioning tease. "Watch yourself," she cautioned with a step back. "Have we had too much to drink?"

"What are you worried about?" she laughed, quickly closing the final step.

Deanne noticed her eyes shift once to something behind

her. Before Deanne could turn to see what it was, Kasey spread her hands out to the side. Her intent became clear when they were met there, clasped from behind by familiar hands.

Four bracelets told the rest, as Sage's body slid against Deanne's back, cradling her rhythmically between pelvis and thighs. Her legs went weak beneath her. "You're beautiful," Sage whispered against her ear. Words spoken to probably a hundred women, yet they made her smile, and sent a sharp twinge through her body.

Kasey brought Sage's hands down and around Deanne, before releasing them. The look she received was a gentle warning from Deanne. "I'm helping you get better acquainted," Kasey winked.

"I don't need any help, thank you," replied Deanne. She turned out of Sage's gentle embrace, and faced her. "You could have asked."

"For a dance? You would have . . . declined."

"I've danced with practically everyone else."

"Then I'm asking now." She stood elegantly poised, outstretched palms inviting the dance, as k.d. lang pleaded "Save Me".

Ignore the words of the song, Deanne warned herself, the ones etching their reference across your heart like a warning label. *Ignore this turmoil, swelling in your body like storm water at its brink. Concentrate on what is real, the promise to never again sell your soul for so cheap a price. Remember, that this time, you may not be able to buy it back.*

With warnings safely in place, Deanne stepped forward. Pulling her eyes from Sage's magnetic stare, she placed her palms against Sage's, and brought their bodies within inches. The heat traveled like an electric current through her body, from her hands, down her arms, through her chest, and settling deep below her abdomen. She felt like a child playing with fire, touching the tips of the flame just long enough to feel the warmth, not enough to feel the pain.

Their bodies swayed around the notes, connected only by the touch of their palms. Inadvertently Deanne's thigh grazed against smooth warm leather, her breast brushed below Sage's. *How long can you play with fire before getting burned?* Sage's eyes bore into the side of Deanne's head, demanding they be met. The test quickened Deanne's heartbeat. She met Sage's eyes, stared directly into the heart of the flame and faced the seduction head-on. She found exactly what she had expected — the look that contradicted all reason, the look that made her forget who she was and where she was. Her heart was pounding so hard that she feared it would bridge the tiny gap between them and beat against Sage's chest. Her eyes, she worried, may be giving away what her body was saying silently.

Deanne broke eye contact, unwilling to tempt fate even a second longer. Sage's lips touched lightly against her temple. "Let's take the next four hours," she whispered into wispy strands of honey gold, "and let this excitement take its natural course. When we're only a breath away from ecstasy, let's hang on to that breath, until taking it together is all that exists."

Deanne's breath caught somewhere before exhale, a shock the size of a thunderbolt shooting straight through her chest. She closed her eyes and allowed her head for only an instant to press into the waiting lips. She took a slow, steady breath, trying to recover. She relied on what always seemed to work for her. "Is that the line that makes the poor damsel fall helplessly into your arms?" She chanced a look up. "Blinded by lust for her single night of ecstasy?"

"Is it?"

"No. It isn't," she said, with a shred more composure. "It is a valiant effort, though. Maybe I'll use it in a book some-time."

"Maybe you'd rather I be more direct and tell you that I want you . . . that I want to make love to you."

"Well, since I want a friend and a lover, one who loves me

enough to spend the rest of their life with me, it looks like one of us is destined for disappointment." She backed away, slipping her hand from Sage's. "Thank you for the dance."

The jockeying began subtly at 11:45 and became noticeably serious at 11:55. Women, with plans of laying claim to Sage's lips at the witching hour, kept conversations short and Sage in view. The likes of Amelia Earhart, Wonder Woman, and the First Lady, were all more than willing to begin the New Year in Sage's arms, in Sage's bed.

Sage, dedicated to her own agenda, continued moving, making her way steadily toward the stairs. At 11:59 she found what she was looking for. Deanne came hurriedly down the stairs; Sage started up, halting Deanne's descent near the bottom. Their silence was awkward. Sage's hand found Deanne's waist.

"I'm looking for Jodie."

Sage removed her hand and stepped aside. "Then that's who you'll find."

Sage was curiously absent for the countdown, unavailable for the celebration kiss. Hugs all around were a disappointing substitute for each woman who was sure she would have been the chosen one. Deanne and Jodie, arms still around one another, made their excuses and said good night.

With a little luck, Deanne thought, she'd be out the door before Sage reappeared. She pulled on her boots and retrieved her coat from the closet.

"Are you leaving?"

It could never be so easy. She faced Sage in the darkened entranceway. "Yes. Jodie's warming the car."

"Stay, and let me take you home."

Deanne shook her head. "I came with Jodie, and I'll leave with her."

"Is that what you want to do?"

Deanne turned toward the door. "That's what I'm going to do."

Sage took her arm and turned her. "Why are you dating her?" The riveting eyes seemed to plead for honesty.

"We've been good friends for years. She's kind and considerate —"

"And low risk."

Deanne wasn't going to respond to that. It would mean denying it; defending it would be too exhausting. Yet as hard as she tried hiding the truth her eyes gave her away.

Sage read their meaning easily. She took Deanne's hand and gently pulled her closer.

Deanne felt her hand being lifted and placed inside the low opening of Sage's blouse. Her palm pressed to the warm delicate skin between her breasts. She stared into Sage's eyes and knew she should pull away; but she could not. Her fingers lay nervously against the tempting swell of Sage's breast.

"What should I do about this?" Sage asked, her heart pounding its rhythm hard against the captive palm. She watched Deanne's eyes lower to her hand.

This seductress was for real. There were no fairy tales here, no secondhand stories. She was real, staring into her, making her flesh melt. This was not a joke she could laugh off. No, this was not going to be that easy. For Deanne, this could be no game. Sage Bristo could not have this statistic, not as long as Deanne's mind was stronger than her body. And, as long as it was, she would stave off this attempt, and the next, and the next, until Sage tired of it. She would overcome what this was doing to her body. The heat, the wetness. She would.

Sage lifted the still unresisting hand once again, this time to her lips. Their softness burned into Deanne's palm. The emotion that drew Sage's eyes closed seemed so sincere.

God! This was hard. So very hard to keep her hand from slipping around the proud neck, and allowing her body to dissolve into her embrace. Nearly impossible to keep from tasting the lips, which surely meant giving in to them. But, she would. She had to.

At the sound of the door behind her, Deanne quickly retrieved her hand from Sage's lips. Jodie poked her head in the door, covered in fresh snow. "Ready Dee? Bundle up, it's snowing like crazy. Happy New Year, Sage."

Deanne gave Sage not a word, not even a glance. The door closed decisively behind her.

Chapter 20

Thick heavy flakes accumulated quickly into a soft white blanket, covering the car as it sat in the drive. Heat, blasting full force from the vents, immediately turned the flakes into little streams of water that worked their way erratically down the windshield.

"I was right about Sage having her sights on you, wasn't I?"

"Nothing's changed, Jodie. I told you I turned her down right at the beginning." Deanne was trying not to be annoyed at her; after all, she couldn't know how uncomfortable Sage made her feel. And Jodie certainly didn't live in a bubble. She undoubtedly had felt uneasy herself.

"I sensed something when we were leaving. At the risk of

sounding possessive, which I don't want to do, may I ask what it was?"

"You have a right to know; I was your date tonight. She asked me to stay and let her take me home. Jodie, don't be jealous of someone like her. I'm only a challenge to her, that's all. I know that. She isn't used to a woman who doesn't drop at her feet."

"It's enough that she has killer looks . . . but money, too. Tips the scale pretty heavily in her favor."

"I'm here with you."

"Yes." Jodie slid from behind the wheel, pleased at her decision to keep the old Buick with its 60/40 seat.

"Then, she has something to be jealous of you about, doesn't she?" Smiling, she welcomed Jodie's embrace, which was somewhat hampered by cumbersome jackets. Their tender kisses soon reached the limit Deanne had set over the past weeks, but a more confident Jodie began challenging that limit. She pressed a little harder, embraced a little tighter. Deanne surprised her when she relented, parting her lips and kissing her back, then shocking her by opening her jacket to allow her hands inside.

Jodie's kisses traveled to the deepest part of Deanne's neck, below her collar, while her hands warmly roamed the material of her sweatsuit. "Let's go inside," she whispered.

Deanne stroked Jodie's coarse graying hair and spoke softly. "I want you to make love to me."

Excitement, mixed with astonishment, overwhelmed her. "Oh, Dee," she whispered, trying to contain the emotion. "I've wanted this for so long." But when she felt Deanne unzipping her sweatsuit, Jodie knew she meant here in the car, not under fresh sheets lying naked against Deanne's finely toned body smelling pure and sweet. Yet how could she deny her hands, already exploring beneath the layers, the chance they had now? Or her lips their opportunity? After all, it was she searching out the warmth of Deanne Demore; her mouth tasting the sweet tenderness of her breast. Not Sage Bristo's.

"Jodie, that feels so nice."

"Deanne," she spoke so carefully, "you know I love you."

"Yes, I know."

Jodie felt the words whispered against her head and ignored that they spoke not of love. The wetness she felt, as her hand slid into the panties, was enough for now. She stroked gently, expressed her love tenderly with her lips. The murmurs, she knew, were for her.

Deanne's movements increased in urgency. She pressed Jodie's mouth tighter to her breast. "Make me come to you, Jodie. I need to come to you."

She moved with her, and guided her, and for a while Jodie's tenderness felt good. But when the wetness Sage had created disappeared, a sensitivity took its place. She tried to hurry Jodie, guiding her in and moving against her. Attempts to block Sage's face from her mind were futile, and closing her eyes only made it more difficult. Thoughts of Sage wouldn't leave. Her scent remained, despite Deanne burying her face in Jodie's hair. Deanne covered Jodie's hand and stilled her. If she could not come to Jodie, she would not come to Sage Bristo.

"You made me feel so good, Jodie, so loved." She held Jodie tightly against her, stroking her head lovingly.

"I want to spend the night with you, so I can feel you lying next to me, so I can love you like you should be loved."

"Not tonight."

Alone, Sage lay face up on the bed, one arm draped over her eyes. Covering them did nothing to keep the visions from coming. Visions of Deanne in Jodie's arms; exactly where she had chased her. Deanne's mouth hungrily accepting Jodie's kisses. Jodie's hands quickly stripping away her clothes, touching where only a lover could touch. The woman she wanted so much, aroused to heights of passion, pleading for the release of orgasm. A release Sage would give her, sweet and full, if only her hands could be where Jodie's were, if only her mouth was allowed visitation to that remarkable body.

The vision was torturous, bringing a pain she hadn't experienced before. It was a feeling so intense, that it easily surpassed that of physical pain, challenging even that of loneliness. She tried to stiffen against it. Only her body responded. The process that over the years had become automatic should have begun by now. Blocking out the pain, preserving her objectivity, keeping her safe. Let it be, she reminded herself. Just let it be. Let what you cannot change be. She tried to start the process consciously. *This will pass. Pain is only fleeting. It will pass.* It always had.

Sage turned her face into the dampness of her pillow, erasing the evidence of tears, unable to bring an uncooperative heart under control.

Chapter 21

Deanne lay snuggled beneath the heavy old quilt, her arms wound tightly around her pillow. She stretched lazily in the warmth, closed her eyes, and snuggled deeper into her cocoon. Despite her physical comfort, she had slept very little. Her distressed mind had prolonged the inevitable only to a reasonable hour. Reluctantly, she reached for the phone and hit the automatic dial button.

"Jodie Brandt," came the cheerful voice on the other end.

"I'm coming over. I need to talk to you."

* * * * *

Jodie met her at the door with her usual smile, and handed her a glass of juice. "Come, sit down, breakfast is ready."

Making eye contact was uncomfortable, but Deanne forced herself. Such smooth youthful skin, she admired. *If she'd only color her hair, she'd look so young.* Jodie, however, was free of burdensome afflictions such as 'age-phobias'. She didn't care to tamper with the natural course of things; there were more important issues in life, like staying alcohol-free. Respect for Jodie was making Deanne's purpose even harder. Considering Jodie's struggle always put her own in perspective. "You're not going to want to feed me after what I have to say."

Jodie sat facing her across the table, sipping her coffee thoughtfully. Dark blue eyes bore into Deanne's momentarily, then relented and softened. "DeDe, I know you're not in love with me. It's something that's not easily faked, at least by you."

The relief was immediate. Deanne rested her forehead in her hands and said nothing. Jodie appeared beside her chair. Lovingly, she gathered Deanne's head in her hands, and gently pulled her against her. "I think I let myself believe you could be, for a while there, but deep inside I've known," she said quietly.

"I'm sorry." Deanne wrapped her arms around the thin hips, and rested her face against the old blue flannel. "I knew how you felt. I took advantage of it. I was sure I'd ruined our friendship," she said, tightening her arms and blotting her tears.

"It would take a lot more than that," she replied. Her soothing fingers traced through Deanne's hair. "Our friendship's strong enough for that; you knew it, or you wouldn't have been able to see me today, maybe not for a long time."

Deanne wiped her eyes. "Why is life so weird? If there was anyone in this world I should be in love with, it's you." Her eyes held concern, and met Jodie's as she released her.

"You can't make things like that happen. If it were possi-

ble, we'd have been together long before you and Angie were."
She took Deanne's plate and placed it in the microwave, while
Deanne marveled silently at how long her most loyal friend
had loved her. Over six years that she was aware of.

"I'd have treated you a whole lot better, too."

"You have. And I've often thought about what my life
would have been like with you instead of Angie. What's my
problem?"

Jodie leaned against the counter and stared seriously at
the woman she loved. Sunlight streamed through the hair
that she teasingly called Dee's version of a tamed Tina
Turner. *Such untapped talent in this woman, such love un-
appreciated.* How she cherished her. "She's going to tear your
heart right out of your chest."

The warning was somewhat startling. "I can't be her lover,
any more than I can be yours. The reasons are different,
but . . ." The warmed breakfast was a welcomed diversion.

"I've seen how you look at her," Jodie offered between
bites.

"How?"

"Like a moonstruck teenager. You flush when you know
she's watching you."

"I do not."

"You do. You're flushing now."

"You're embarrassing me." She refocused on her plate,
while the heat from her face spread down her neck.

"I'm having a hard time being objective here; I'll admit
that. But I don't think you're being objective, either. You
might be saying all the right words, but I suspect a whole
different thing is going on inside. Am I right?"

"I am being objective. I haven't lost sight of the fact that
my age makes attention from someone like Sage Bristo very
flattering. And I've never attempted a relationship based on
anything so precarious as flattery. I never would have been
with Angie if that were the case. God, what's that telling me?"

"Only that falling in love, or lust, can make fools out of

139

the best of us. She wasn't right for you for a lot of reasons, but you just couldn't see it. What was most scary, though, is that you stayed even after you did see it."

"It was good at first. She was very sweet. It deteriorated so gradually; I didn't recognize what was happening. I only felt the results. To be fair, I have to shoulder half the blame."

"I don't think so, Dee, unless it would be for not leaving sooner." She drew dishwater, while Deanne cleared the dishes from the table. Jodie's tone turned noticeably sour. "What I think irritates me most, Deanne, is that you still refuse to call her the selfish asshole that she is. After all the times you had to hide out here to write. All the lies and the guilt. For what? So that you could exercise your God-given gift, so that you could nurture yourself. I couldn't stand it."

"I'm sorry, Jodie. I burdened you for so long."

Her voice softened considerably. "It wasn't a burden," she said, looking into Deanne's eyes. "I watched my happy, out-going friend become a depressed social recluse who spent most of her energy trying not to upset her partner. You don't know how painful that was for me. I won't be able to watch you go through that again."

"I'm finally healthy. I have no intention of putting myself in that position again." Dishtowel in hand, she waited for Jodie to rinse the dishes.

"Even if I wasn't in love with you, I'd be worried. I think Sage has been around the block so many times she could make the trip faster in her sleep than I could on the Honda." Although the subject was a painful one, Jodie wanted to see her friend smile, and she did. The one that started in her eyes, and ended in an easy laugh. An anxious pleasure for Jodie; like the enjoyment of watching a beautiful bird, you knew was only resting a short time on your windowsill. She would enjoy it while she could. "You're finally laughing like your old self again. You don't have to worry about pleasing anyone now, Deanne, except you. You're free to spend your time reading, writing, or working out — however you wish. Anyone who doesn't appreciate you for who you are can take a walk," she smiled. "You need to be surrounded with positives."

"I've done that; and it feels good."

"And, so does Sage."

"You think she's going to snap her fingers, and I'm going to disengage my brain and jump in bed with her?"

"I think if you did, it wouldn't mean the same thing for her as it would to you. Women like her have recreational sex. They get to home plate, mark up the score, and start thinking about their next time up."

"You don't have any more respect for my intelligence than Angie did." The anger, heard in her words, had taken years to surface, but now that it had, she expressed it almost too easily.

"That's not true, Deanne. You know better than that. It's your heart, your emotional sensitivity, that makes me worry."

"Was that what you were worried about last night?" Subduing the anger had become more difficult to do, even anger as unjustified as this.

Jodie, never one to hide her emotion, let it show in her eyes. "That's not fair, and you know it."

The hurt Deanne saw there, did what she could not do on her own. It immediately extinguished the anger. "No, it's not . . . I don't mean to hurt you, Jodie." She smiled a repentant smile. "Maybe we should get married. We fight like an old married couple, and probably love each other just as deeply."

"If I ever think you truly mean that, you won't have to ask twice."

"I haven't meant to take you for granted, you know. I have been too wrapped up in my own situation, my own unhappiness, to notice how painful our friendship had become for you." She looked up from the dishtowel, and the fringe she had meticulously straightened. "Forgive me for being so selfish, Jodie. I always knew you were there, caring about me, supporting me. They would have signed me into the fourth-floor ward had it not been for your wisdom and strength. I don't think I can adequately tell you what your friendship has meant. But if it's become too painful, you have to tell me."

"Sometimes I almost hate you for how I feel. I used to hope for the next argument bad enough to send you here in the middle of the night. Then I'd spend days fighting the guilt your anguish over it caused me. I'd look at the tears in your eyes and vow that I'd do anything to take them away. I just wanted you to be happy, even if it wasn't with me, even if it meant going back to Angie." Deanne took Jodie's hands and held them. The expression in the dark blue eyes was a bittersweet reminder of what the early days had held, before the anger, before the strengthening had begun. It had been a long trip from there. Jodie looked at her, eyes moist with emotion. "I can even tell you the exact time that I knew that you had changed me forever."

"Tell me."

"Remember the figurine your grandmother gave you?"

Deanne nodded. "The one Angie broke when she was mad, because she knew how much it meant to me."

"When you showed up at my door, with all the pieces in a box." She looked down and squeezed Deanne's hands.

"You spent hours helping me glue it all back together."

"I knew, watching you so carefully placing the pieces together, that I'd lost my heart to you."

Tears were streaming down Deanne's face. "You kept it for me all those years, loved me all those years."

"I always will, wherever you are, whomever you're with."

Chapter 22

A stunning array of summer color complemented the lush greenery and spilled over the rocks of the gardens that lined the paths of the Longhouse atrium. Deanne sharpened the focus on the hand-ground lens of her Hassey and released the shutter. The afternoon was perfect. A flood of natural sunlight poured from the long glass peak of the atrium ceiling, heightening the brilliance of blues and purples and reds. The pictures would be absolutely postcard perfect, as much to the credit of the designer as to her photographic skills.

She was glad she had accepted the job, despite its uncomfortable resemblance to the irresistible carrot being dangled before the horse. Maybe she would bring Mom and Dad for a tour after all. The entire complex of homes and gardens was an impressive undertaking, resulting in an environment most could only dream about. She had to admit, she felt a certain amount of pride knowing that it was Sage's concept and Kasey's contractual skills that had created such a remarkable place. She snapped another frame before heading up the sloped path to the mezzanine for lunch.

She found Sage and Cimmie at a private table overlooking the south leg of the gardens. The sound of water trickling happily over the rocks and splashing into natural little pools below created instant calm. It turned out to be the most stress-free job she'd ever taken, and it showed in her face.

"Sage, this place is incredible. I am duly impressed."

Sage directed her comment to Cimmie. "I had to hire her to get her out here."

"Stop," Deanne laughed. "I'd have been out here, sooner or later."

"I would have preferred sooner."

"Did you get some good pictures?" Cimmie asked.

"My Aunt Margaret could take good pictures here, and she hasn't taken one yet with all heads present and accounted for."

Genuine amusement radiated from the smile spreading the width of Cimmie's face. Deanne relaxed completely in its warm acceptance. In the course of two hours, they had found a camaraderie that normally takes months to develop. Cimmie was easy to like. She was open and ingenuous in conversation and freely animated in her expressions. The light to Sage's darkness. The sisters provided a fascinating study in contrast, and an enlightening view of complementary personalities. Deanne was enjoying every minute of it.

"Don't let her fool you," Sage was saying. "She's a feature writer for newspapers and a statewide magazine. Plus, she's written I don't know how many short stories. By the way, did you know your father let me read one?"

"I suspected as much. He's a proud father. But I'm afraid he lacks objectivity."

"Then I must, too. I love the way you write. I don't know how, in so few pages, you took me so deeply into your characters."

"Are you published?" Cimmie asked.

Deanne shook her head. "Two attempts, two rejections. It's quite a humbling process."

"Is that all? You haven't gotten your feet wet, yet. You're going to keep trying, aren't you?"

The young woman serving their lunch removed their salad plates, and began serving the main course. "It's been years since I've had the confidence to do that. Sage, as much as I love lasagna, I can't eat it."

"Ah, but you can — and the cheesecake we're having for dessert. They've been specially prepared without lactose."

"Ooh, I'd given up satisfying that craving long ago. This is all very thoughtful, Sage."

"It so happens that lasagna is Cimmie's favorite, too."

"And between us, we've devoured many a cheesecake," added Cimmie. "On quiet evenings, when each other's company was more important than a date."

"So anytime you'd care to satisfy a craving, let me know," smiled Sage.

Cimmie smiled at what she suspected was another moderately subtle come on by her sister. It was confirmed when Deanne avoided her eyes. In all their years, she'd never actually seen her sister in action. It was a show she was taking great delight in.

Diplomatic, Deanne mused. All the little come ons today had been carefully placed within polite conversation, emerging nicely from the natural flow of the neatly arranged schedule. Cimmie was much too aware not to have noticed. Yet even that was okay. She liked Cimmie a lot; Deanne felt completely at ease in her company. Cimmie's feelings for her sister were so apparent that without even realizing it, Deanne had begun to experience Sage through her. Love through Cimmie was unchallenged, loyalty was unquestioned. Gone were all signs of reservation and guarded emotion and even suspicions of insincerity that normally burdened Deanne's mind when she was around Sage. She was experiencing a wonderfully refreshing view of Sage Bristo. She planned to enjoy that view even if it lasted for only a day.

"Hmm, I'll be right back," Deanne said. "I see something I like." She gathered her camera and tripod, and scurried off toward the edge of the mezzanine.

Cimmie smiled. "And so do you, dear sister." She was watching Sage's eyes as they followed Deanne's retreating figure. They came slyly back and rested comfortably in Cimmie's gaze.

"It shows, doesn't it?"

"Being anal doesn't account for the care you've taken all day or the smile you can't keep off your face. There's got to be something happening when her eyes meet yours, because I've never seen you look like that."

"That's because I've never felt like this."

"Sage!" Cimmie exclaimed with a surprised smile the width of her face. "Come on, big sister. I've been waiting a long time for this!"

With a sigh, Sage leaned back and draped one arm over the back of her chair. "You're reveling in this, aren't you?"

"Thoroughly."

She shook her head and sighed again. "God, Cim, I'm so full of her. She's all I think about. Her eyes shoot into me like a stun gun. Her smile drops me to my knees."

"Oh, Sage! Have you told her? Have you slept with her?" Cimmie asked excitedly.

"Yes, and no. I've tried to tell her, but I haven't so much as kissed her."

"You haven't slept with her and you feel like this? This is better than I thought. I always imagined you'd fall hard, but this," she giggled. "This is like a canoe going over Niagara Falls."

Sage's face lost its earlier joy. "It's going to be a painful

146

fall. She's not interested in anything beyond being euchre partners."

"I don't know if I'd run to the bank with that one, if I were you." She motioned with her eyes that Deanne was re-joining them.

"How did my dessert survive alone, between you two cheesecake hounds?"

Cimmie pointed to fresh water drops on the tablecloth. "Drool marks," she said. "You were cutting it close."

Deanne laughed and squeezed her hand.

"How's your dad doing, Deanne?" Sage asked.

"Amazingly well. He's using the scooter on his bad days. Mom has been following the special diet your dietitian sent."

"We have arthritic residents that swear by the results of that diet."

"We appreciate your help, Sage. But I need to know how much I owe you."

"Nothing."

"Don't argue with me. How much do those things rent for?"

"Why can't you just let me do something nice?"

"Then I'm not taking any money for today."

"Yes you are."

"All right, hold it, you two." Cimmie raised her hands to signal peace. "Deanne, as long as the scooter is an extra one, accept it as a loan. And Sage, pay for the cost of her film, and accept Deanne's services."

Deanne looked at Sage. "She's good."

Sage nodded a grin in the direction of her sister, and ex-tended her hand to Deanne in agreement. "That she is."

"Excuse me. Ms. B?" A young woman politely approached the table. "I'm sorry to interrupt your lunch, but I need to talk to you."

"You're sure this is something you can't handle yourself."

"Yes. I wouldn't disturb you unless —"

"All right. It's no problem. Excuse me, ladies."

Cimmie stifled a smile. "We'll be right here . . . Ms B."

"Look at her," Cimmie said, when the two were out of earshot. "Do you think there's any doubt around here about who's in charge?"

"I almost expected to see a puddle on the floor where the poor girl was standing."

Cimmie giggled and began digging in her purse. "Give me one word you think best describes my sister."

"Only one? Hmm, that might be impossible. Maybe *polished*?"

"*Proud, arrogant, seductive*. Just a few others I've heard. *Polished* is good." She slipped a picture from her wallet. "She's a master businesswoman."

"That's two words."

"What do you think her staff would do if they saw this?" Cimmie giggled again and handed Deanne an old color snapshot. "Sage Bristo, sophisticated New York businesswoman."

Deanne began to laugh immediately, and when Cimmie joined her, she laughed even harder. "Long hair?" she blurted, as the two huddled in near hysterics.

The long flowing waves of semi-sweet brown, on a young Sage of seven or eight, would have been enough to make her smile. But the rest of the picture was a comedy in paradox. "The family rule," explained Cimmie, wiping tears from her eyes, "was dress clothes all day Sunday. We never understood why. A neighbor caught Marshall Sage in action, after she captured her fugitive son." Deanne couldn't stop laughing. Young Marshall Sage, gun belt strapped about her waist, skinned knee propped upon the porch step, held her captive with the skirt of her pink flowered dress wrapped around his neck.

It was too much. Deanne couldn't remember the last time she had laughed so hard. She wiped tears from her cheeks. "Just massaged that stupid rule right into something useful."

"You have to promise not to tell her you saw this." Cimmie managed between giggles, "at least for a while."

"Shh, shh. She keeps looking over here."

"Oh, Lord. You don't know how many times I've threatened to use this picture. I don't know why now. Something just came over me."

"The laugh has done me a world of good."

Cimmie tucked the picture safely away. "I love my sister dearly. I wish she could enjoy something this much." Cimmie's smile dissolved into pensiveness. "There hasn't been much room for joy in her life. With all my heart, I hope that's changing."

"Having you here obviously makes her happy. There's something extraordinary between you."

"My sister and I are survivors, Deanne. We've always found what we needed in each other — strength, compassion. But we still had to find our own way to overcome. Our paths eventually had to separate; the path to happiness has to be traveled alone." Cimmie looked adoringly in the direction of her sister. "My path's always been the easier one, partly because of Sage. From as young as I can remember, she would do everything a little girl could do to take the pain for both of us." Deanne watched the look in Cimmie's eyes travel the distance in time and pain. "Sage would wrap herself around me and turn her back to the wrath of our father. I can still feel the jolts from the blows to her body, and I was the one crying." This time the tears Deanne saw in her eyes, she knew, were born of a love tempered by the fire of tremendous emotional pain. The depth of such a love was unfathomable.

Silence hung poignantly between them, saying much more than words ever could. Deanne covered Cimmie's hand with her own and held it tightly. "There is someone special for her," Cimmie said with a gentle smile. "She deserves someone special."

Sage's long, sure stride brought her quickly up the mezzanine slope. Cimmie added quickly. "She keeps everything to herself. If there are things you need to know, you'll have to ask her."

149

* * * * *

A fresh light snow covered the old footprints and crunched beneath their boots. Sage and Deanne strode casually along the path leading away from the residents' houses.

"Cimmie had some phone calls to make, but she made me promise to show you the lake."

"This whole place boggles my mind. You have every right to be proud of what you've accomplished."

"It's a tribute to my grandmother, true to our heritage as *Hodinonhsonik,* house builders. It was her money that built it. And Kasey. Without her, I'd have been lost."

"I can't imagine that. You being lost, I mean."

Sage's smile was fresh, almost sweet. "Do you mind if we have company on our walk?"

Deanne looked up at the source of the strange footsteps. The big bay quickened his pace at Sage's encouragement. "Niio walks with me every day. He's a wonderful listener. You can tell him anything, and he keeps it discreetly to himself," she smiled. "A perfect gentleman." Her strokes, to the flat plane between the big brown eyes, received an appreciative nudge in return. "He'll even carry you home on his back when you're tired."

"He's beautiful." Deanne stroked the velvet nose. "And very handsome in all his winter finery."

Sage smiled at the maroon-and-green coat strapped around his huge back. "He had a rough life before I found him. Now he gets the best there is."

"What did you call him?"

"*Niio.* In Iroquoian it means, 'So be it'. Do you believe in omens, Deanne?"

"I guess so."

"Niio was my omen. He was a most gracious host. From his back, he showed me the beauty of this land. We rode until we were exhausted, and I knew this is where I was supposed to be."

"Okay. I'm fascinated. Tell me more." Deanne waited. When Sage was slow to respond, she prodded her along. "I had guessed your lineage as Italian."

"You're partially correct. My grandmother was full Seneca."

"The one that all this is about?" Sage nodded and stroked Niio's powerful neck. "What was she like?"

"The wisest woman I've ever known. She came from a powerful heritage of Seneca women. The women governed the longhouses, raised the crops, and reared the children. They chose and disposed" — she raised an eyebrow in emphasis — "the male *sachems*, 'chiefs', of the clans. They even decided whether prisoners of war were to be adopted or put to death. Their decision was based on how they ran a gauntlet of women." Sage turned and smiled at Deanne. "I've often wondered if I was born into the wrong time. I think you would have liked NaNan Bristo. She would have been a shaman to her people, a holy woman, mystical and wise. The values she held dear would make us all better people."

"You develop very special bonds, don't you?"

"She raised me and loved me. She kept my soul safe from harm. She saved my life."

"How?"

"My father would have eventually killed me, or I him." She motioned toward the lake, as they reached the top of the crest.

Before them lay a vast expanse of frozen tranquility, Mother Nature dressed in her finest winter wardrobe. A soft blanket of virgin snow blended the definition between forest and shore, rock and water. Snow-laden boughs of deep green drooped gracefully from giant pines. Warmed by the afternoon sun, a large clump of snow slid from a bough as they watched, falling into pieces that dimpled the soft blanket below. Low in the sky, the late sun glistened across the winter landscape.

"Mother Nature's showing off." Deanne smiled. "I should have brought my camera."

"I won't touch this part. It'll stay as Mother Nature wishes, except for the house. It's supposed to be built there, on the north shore. Kasey's getting impatient with me. I still haven't chosen the plans."

"If I had the money to build any house I wanted, I'd be so excited —"

"An expensive house isn't necessarily a home. To be that, it has to be shared in love, along with this," she indicated the view before them, "and the rose-colored dawns."

Sage talked of a value, ancient and true, so overlooked in a world that judges the quality of life by its monetary value. Deanne allowed the silence to lie undisturbed between them. She sensed a loneliness that surprised her. She continued looking out over the lake, blowing into her bare hands to warm them.

"Here," Sage said, removing her gloves and handing them to her.

Deanne slid her hands into the warm, butter-soft leather. "This time I won't argue with you. Thank you." They smiled in amusement at the leftover leather at the ends of the fingers. "What do you think your grandmother would say if she saw this place?"

Sage scanned the beautiful landscape. "NaNan expected perfection from nature. She had an innate appreciation of it. She would touch everything in the gardens and sink her fingers into the soil. She knew it was *human* nature that couldn't be depended upon. From me, she would have expected no less, and no more, than my best. When she had taken it all in, she would have straightened her proud shoulders, looked me straight in the eyes, and said, 'You have done well'. Of course, she would promptly remind me that we do not own the land, that we are caretakers." Sage dropped her gaze, a slight smile on her lips but sadness in her eyes. "Then, she'd take my hand in hers and tell me the stories of the real longhouses, and of the women whose clans bore their names. She'd tell me of the woman warrior who came to her in dreams, who fought alongside the men to protect her people."

A fleeting figure dashed across Deanne's mind, and vanished before she could identify it. She tried to retrieve it, but could not. It had happened before, and each time it left her feeling strangely anxious. This time however as she looked at Sage, the anxiety was countered by a stronger feeling. She was stunned by an awareness of the deep sentiment and love this woman held. She remembered the night of the question game, the look she'd seen in Sage's eyes after speaking of her grandmother, and the unexpected concern she had felt for her then. "I'm sad that I'll never get to meet her. I feel like I want to know everything about her. Actually, you make me feel like I do know her. I wish I could write her stories. It's very important that they be preserved, so that others can share them."

"The Indian traditionally passed them down to the next generation verbally, through the stories of the elders. That's how I will pass them to Cimmie's children, and hope they will pass them to theirs. But if something happened, that I never get to . . . Could you write them through me?"

"How's your memory?"

"It's all I have left of her. I've taken very good care of it."

"Start carrying a little tape recorder with you. Whenever you think of something, take a minute and —"

"Talk to myself," she smiled.

"No, talk to me, any time of day or night."

"Do we really need the tape recorder?"

"Niio," Deanne rubbed the large curve of his jaw as she spoke. " Your friend here is hopeless."

Chapter 23

Sage pressed her head back, squeezing the coolness from the wet towel rolled around her neck. Halftimes were never long enough any more. She made one more reassuring look at the scoreboard, before rejoining her teammates for the last of the warm-up shots. Two points up meant nothing really — only the promise of a harder-fought battle in the second half.

Towel still around her neck, she was greeted at the free-throw line with a ball and Chinita's toothy smile. "Where did Sharon come up with all that sweetness tonight?" she asked.

With a puzzled look, Sage followed her gaze to the bleachers.

"She picked herself up three pounds of sugar. She gonna share that with us?"

Sage grinned. She was not surprised that Chinita was more interested in checking out beautiful women than winning a basketball game, even a championship game, with only one sub on the bench. Nor was she surprised that the diversion was refreshing. "Not exactly for us," she answered. "The two in the middle are married."

Chinita took a pass and sank a lazy jumper. "A night out with the lesbians?"

"No, married to each other." Sage swished another free throw.

"What?" Chinita looked again to the bleachers, as Kasey and Connie stood to stretch their legs. "Aw, no." She crinkled one side of her face. "Shit like that should be against lesbian law. Wastin' that on each other. Huh-uh. Honey that good's supposed to be spread and licked by many."

"You're a sick lesbian, Chinita, but that's why you're our queen." Sage playfully tapped a ball away from her and shot it. "No one talks smut like you do."

Chinita laughed and waved at Deanne.

"You know Deanne?"

"Uh-huh." She snatched a ball from in front of Sage. "Best point guard in the league about five years ago. Got a helluva jumper. She could shoot your eyes out."

"Yeah?" Sage looked toward the bleachers, a rebound just missing her head. "I've been trying to date her for months."

As the blaring of the buzzer called them back to battle, Chinita chided. "Maybe she's looking for something a little taller and a little darker."

Sage shoved the ball back hard at her. "You can just get that notion out of your nappy ol' head."

"This is really the first time you've seen the ice queen play?" asked Kasey.

Deanne mused at the appropriateness of the term. "I see

155

her name in the paper all the time but never made it to a game." She returned her attention more intently to the court. Something about the way Sage moved tried to take her mind somewhere else. Somewhere she knew she'd been, but couldn't recall. Flickers of the memory escaped her. Sage crossed the centerline in full stride. The stride was familiar to her, with the length of a fine racehorse and the urgency of a messenger carrying the weight of life or death.

"I told you she was good," Sharon added.

"I never doubted that she was."

Connie reclaimed her seat and joined the conversation. "I love to watch her shoot. It doesn't seem physically possible for her to stay suspended in the air that long."

The second half of the game gathered momentum as the women discussed the attributes of the Sychrocees top scorer. "What I find fascinating, besides the excitement of the game, are the skills she has that can't be taught," explained Deanne.

"Like what?" asked Sharon.

"Watch this next shot. Watch her shooting elbow." They waited in anticipation until once again the ball was passed to Sage after a diagonal cut through the key. She pivoted into a jump shot that sent a perfectly rotating shot through the hoop. "See the placement of her elbow, right in front of her face like that? Impossible to block without fouling. And the follow-through, off her fingers, straight through the basket. That gives the ball that nice soft roll. That's technique — good technique — that can be taught and coached." Connie watched Deanne closely as she spoke. "But did you notice how she goes up strong, amid all the bumping and slapping and the pressure, and stays her focus right where it should be? That's innate. It can't be taught. That's what makes her the 'ice queen'."

Connie whispered something in Kasey's ear, something that compelled her attention from the excitement on the court, to notice the excitement in Deanne's face. Kasey smiled, and gave an acknowledging nod to another inaudible comment.

A loud blasting of whistles alerted them to the breakup of a skirmish in the opponent's key. The opposing coach stormed the sideline in front of his bench, yelling loudly at the referees. "They got their hands all over my girls. Goddamn queers!"

"Shit! It's gonna get nothin' but rougher from here," predicted Sharon. Her brow wrinkled with concern. "As homophobic as those prima donnas are, they're gonna pull out all the stops to keep from losing to the lezzies two years in a row."

And indeed it did get rougher. Fouls, called and uncalled, were more blatant; confrontations were more frequent. The score continued to seesaw by one and two points. Tempers began to affect the quality of play. After a vicious exchange of hips and elbows in the key, Chinita taunted, "Those love pats mean you're dumpin' your ol' man?"

The opposing defense began collapsing in the key, taking away most of Chinita's inside game, and effectively eliminating the pick and cut for Sage. Only their point guard remained to harass the Sychrocees' outside shooter; and she successfully intimidated her into killing her dribble too early. Suddenly, the Sychrocees were down by five, and things did not look good at the three-minute mark.

A time-out resulted in a strategy change and quickly put them back in the game. A higher pick at the top of the circle and a cut back up to the line by Sage created two outside options. They were down by one with fifty-eight seconds remaining in the game. The crowd of about one hundred of the players' families and friends became almost uncontrollable. The shouts and whistles were deafening. To a person now, friend and foe were on their feet.

Then again, as she had already done too many times, the opposing guard drove the right side of the key, challenging the guard and forward who picked her up, both with four fouls. And once again, her shot banked off the backboard to put them up by three.

"They've got to stop her up high," shouted Deanne. "She can't go to her left."

"Get down there," shouted Sharon with a push. "Hurry! They called a time-out."

Deanne rapidly worked her way down the crowded bleachers and ran across to the huddle of surprised players. Quickly she knelt, and the circle tightened. There were looks full of determination and affirming nods before a blast from the buzzer broke the huddle. Deanne scurried back to the bleachers as the battle-worn warriors took their offensive positions.

A missed shot by the weak-side guard and a long rebound lost put the Sychrocees almost immediately back on defense. But this time, the guards challenged early. When the point guard began her drive to the right, the little dark-haired guard overplayed the ball, forcing her to a weak left hand, and right into the waiting hands of the other guard. With a quick sweep, she tapped the ball out of her dribble and scrambled after to control it. All alone, the little dark-haired guard raced toward the basket. The pass was right on target at the free-throw line, and she easily completed the break to put them within one. The clock showed thirty-six seconds. Immediately her teammates swarmed into a press, not wanting to use up their last time-out. Tremendous hustle from nearly exhausted legs forced their opponents to the limit to in-bound the ball and snatched the resulting pass.

Twenty-nine seconds. They scrambled quickly to offensive positions. The guard with the ball, dribbling, looked to Chinita. The center collapsed, access denied. Pressure on the guard forced a bounce pass to a hustling Sage, not quite in position. She raised the ball, but her position was poor.

The crowd was screaming now. Deanne grabbed Sharon's arm and yelled, "They're going for her feet."

"What?" she yelled back as Sage passed off.

"Her feet — it's the only way to stop her shot."

"Get down there!" she yelled.

Deanne pushed her way down the bleachers and made it to the bottom as the ball came back to Sage. She stood, help-lessly, as Sage pivoted into position, only to have a foot come down hard on her right instep. Her balance gone, her body twisted and fell back hard to the floor. The ball slipped from her hands. A wild scramble ensued while Sage writhed in pain. Out of the tangled mass, came the little dark-haired guard, snapping the ball into protective custody. Chinita shouted and signaled for their final time-out. A bright yellow nine glared tauntingly from the scoreboard.

Friend and trainer Barb Hanslett was already at Sage's feet. "Let me get your shoe off, Sage," she said, trying to position the right foot.

"I'm fine, I'm fine. Just leave it," Sage demanded.

"Let me look at it."

"I'm fine, I said. I just have to walk it off."

"If you're thinking about playing, forget it!" She looked into the steel-brown stare. "It's stupid, Sage. It could be broken."

"I'm playing."

Barb knew her well enough to admit defeat. She went for the compromise. "I've got to tape you."

"There isn't time."

"We'll make time," Chinita promised.

Barb already had the shoe off and with amazing dexterity began one of the fastest tape jobs of her career. Sage nervously watched the scoring table clock tick down the seconds. Just as it was about to expire, "Don't anyone move! Stop where you are," Chinita called out loudly. "I lost a contact."

Loud protests from their opponents went unsatisfied while the Sychrocees dropped to hands and knees in search of the missing contact. A minute later, Barb was helping Sage to her feet. Jaw clenched tightly, Sage stepped cautiously, then tested her foot more aggressively to wild cheers from a very loud group of women. Just then, Chinita suspiciously announced the miraculous find. "Here it is. I got it, I got it!" Popping it into her mouth, then carefully onto her eye, she called, "Let's play!"

"She's really going to play," stated Deanne to the others, now standing with her at the bottom of the bleachers.

"Injured or not, there's not another player you would want to take the last shot of the game," explained Kasey.

That Sage would play on was exactly what Deanne would have predicted. Like so many things lately, it was just one of those things she knew automatically. The veil that clouded Sage's expressions and reactions had somehow vanished. As subtle as they were, Deanne read them easily now. There were even times when, she swore, a movement or a reaction was identical to one she had seen before. Yet she couldn't explain when or where she'd seen her do it. Maybe they reminded her of another player, years ago. Déjà vu, she decided.

All eyes were now riveted, as they had been most of the night, on Sage Bristo as she maneuvered tenuously down the left perimeter of a tight zone. Either arrogance or under-estimation caused the Peppers to pull off the tagging defense they'd had on Sage much of the game. They opted instead to eliminate the high percentage inside shot with its double danger of foul possibility.

The inbound ball was in the sure hands of the little dark-haired guard. Seven seconds. She kept the ball protected, but alive. A look at Chinita's struggling cut through the center. Dribble stopped. Zone collapsing. Pass faked. Four seconds. An untelegraphed pass met Sage's hands precisely as the weak-side screen set. Pivot. No dribble. Two seconds. Painful push off the right foot — up, for the last time, strong and sure. Release, softly rotating. The women held their collective breath. The long harsh sound of the final buzzer drowned the sweet snap of the net, as the last two points of the game fell cleanly through. Game and championship 76-75 to the Sychrocees.

Deanne's eyes watered, as they always did at times like these. The screen had Sage immediately in a bear hug. Echoing shouts of exuberance filled the gymnasium. Fans poured from the bleachers and rushed to the players. Amid all the congratulations and hugs and compliments, Deanne waited patiently a few feet away. She smiled at Chinita's wide grin with the space between her teeth. "Hey, there you are!" she said, grabbing Deanne in a huge hug that took her off her feet. "You're hired coach!"

"You all played so well. Congratulations."

"We're partying Saturday night. You'd better be there," she said as someone else grabbed her.

Then suddenly, like a sappy scene borrowed from a fifty's movie, the players and friends dispersed from in front of her. There, standing less than ten feet away and looking directly at her, was Sage. Firmly, Deanne resisted the impulse to run and hug her, to tell her how courageous she was, to let the emotion flow. Instead she held the captivating eyes, and walked slowly toward her.

"My heroine," she beamed.

"My mentor," Sage replied with a bow.

"You're a coach's dream. On the court, that is."

Sage raised an eyebrow at the qualification. "You can coach me anytime, anyplace."

Deanne broke eye contact. "How's your foot?"

"I know it's there."

"You should have ice on it right now."

"I know. Barb gave me explicit instructions. I had to promise to have it x-rayed tonight to get her to go home."

"You are having it x-rayed," she said, leaving no room for compromise. "Get your things."

"I'm not going anywhere before I take a shower. And who made you boss, anyway?" Sage cocked her head with a pretense of seriousness.

"Chinita," she smiled. "She hired me. So, get movin'."

"Why did you insist on driving? I'm perfectly capable of driving my own vehicle."

"I know what that's going to do, now that they cut the tape off." Deanne looked at the once slim foot, already distorted with swelling under the ice packs.

"This means you either drive the Explorer home and leave me stranded, or we spend the night together."

"I'll have it back first thing in the morning."

"Ms. Bristo?" The low voice of the attending physician broke the intrigue of their private cat-and-mouse game. Sage reluctantly gave him her attention. "We have the results of your X ray. You have a complete fracture of the fifth metatarsal, plus some fairly extensive tearing of the soft tissue in the area of the outer malleolus. We need to get it cast before it swells anymore."

"You have a broken bone and a severely sprained ankle," Deanne interpreted.

"Show me where the break is," Sage directed at neither in particular.

Deanne pointed to the outside edge of her foot. "Exactly," the doctor confirmed.

"Then it won't affect the joint."

"No, the range of movement is affected by the sprain."

"Is the bone displaced?"

"No. Everything seems to line up nicely," he reported.

"Sage, I know where you're going with this," warned Deanne. "Don't make it harder on yourself."

162

"I don't want it cast," she insisted.

"We really should, Ms. Bristo. That way we can insure no displacement and make it easier for you to get around," he explained patiently. "We'll give you a walking cast with a little rubber heel so that when you can stand the weight on it, you won't need the crutches."

"Just wrap it and give me my icing instructions. I'll be fine."

"I strongly recommend casting," the doctor emphasized.

"No."

"Sage, why not?" Deanne asked, slightly frustrated at this point.

"Am I correct, Doctor, that I'll regain full use and strength faster without a cast?"

"Depending on your pain tolerance, I'd have to say yes."

"It's high."

"But the season is over, Sage. Why be miserable?"

"I've been through this before, Deanne, and I don't care to go into it," she said firmly. "I won't be cast."

"Okay," conceded the doctor. "It's your foot, and ultimately your decision."

"Thank you," Sage answered coolly.

Deanne collected extra pillows from the couch while Sage hobbled into the bedroom. "I'm getting ice ready. Yell when you're through changing." She wasn't trying to figure out why Sage refused the cast, maybe it was an independence thing. It didn't matter. It was obviously quite important to her. Deanne also wasn't trying to figure out why she was here, tending to this icon of independence. She knew why. The rationalization that she wanted in some small way to ease her physical discomfort fooled her only briefly. She was here because Sage intrigued her more and more each day. But more truthfully, Sage Bristo, with all her contradictions to commitment and love as Deanne knew it, simply turned her on.

"All right, coach. I'm decent," Sage called.

"That's still a matter of opinion." Deanne smiled at the icon who was sitting as dignified as possible in a gray nightshirt, her foot propped in the air.

Sage gratefully accepted a glass of water and a pain pill. "You know, in spite of your constant barrage of derogatory comments about my character, I'm beginning to think you like me."

"No. It's that I have this vexatious instinctual need to hold small animals and help the injured."

"I suppose I should tell you, then, that having a woman wait on me makes me somewhat uncomfortable."

"Perfect." Deanne secured the ice packs, causing Sage to squirm slightly in discomfort. "Sorry. I know this is starting to get painful. Take that pill if you plan on sleeping at all tonight." She sat on the edge of the bed beside Sage's chair and surveyed her work. When she looked up, she found Sage's eyes surveying her. "You're one hell of an athlete," Deanne said, seriously.

Sage accepted graciously. "Thank you."

"I feel terrible that I didn't get to you in time to warn you. I saw they were going for your feet."

"And heteros say we're rough." She closed her eyes momentarily to mask the pain of readjusting her position. "Chinita's pretty high on your basketball skills. Why did you stop playing?"

"For exactly the reason you got hurt tonight. I was too old to tolerate that kind of play. I got hurt near the end of the season, and that was my last game."

"What happened?"

"Someone undercut me on a fast break. I came down hard. One foot was broken, the other badly sprained." Sage grimaced in sympathy. "I was a true cripple for a while."

"Did you make the basket?"

Deanne laughed. "You're the only one to ever ask that. Yes, I made it."

"My kind of woman," exclaimed Sage. "Why haven't I seen you at any of our games before this?"

"It hasn't been a comfortable place to be. My ex hangs around with a group that still plays."

"What's she like?"

"My ex?"

Sage nodded.

"Miserable."

"Without you?"

"It doesn't matter. She was miserable with me. She's a very unhappy person." She stood and began unwrapping the ice packs. "I think that's good for tonight. Leave the wrap on all night, unless it gets too tight. I'll redo it tomorrow."

"You don't have to do this, Deanne."

"I don't mind," she said, carefully lowering Sage's foot. She offered both hands to help her up.

"You make me feel older than my residents." Sage took her hands. As she stood, Deanne leaned closer than was necessary to offer support. She slipped her arm around Sage's slender waist but stopped when Sage rested her arm around her shoulders. For a long second Deanne hesitated. Sage made not a sound, not a move. The decision was Deanne's.

She turned her head, without eye contact, into the curve of Sage's neck, into the warmth of an embrace she dared to test. She felt the heat of Sage's breath in her hair as she held her motionless against her. She was suddenly aware of holding her breath and of the beating of her heart, as quick as a frightened rabbit frozen in the face of danger. She smelled fresh and clean, a mystery scent lingered from her shower. Sage pressed a kiss gently into her hair. Deanne's senses spun with excitement. *This won't do. It won't do. I'm too old for this nonsense. This is better left alone.*

Deanne separated herself to a more respectable distance.

165

"You'd better get settled," she said, avoiding the eyes she knew would tempt her further. "We're undoing all the good the ice has done."

Sage didn't say a word but lowered herself to the bed. Deanne busied herself placing pillows under Sage's leg and foot, folding back the weight of the heavier covers.

"If I'm not careful," Sage said softly. "I may start enjoying this." She took Deanne's hand as she straightened. "Deanne, thank you."

"I'll be back early. Maybe Sharon can give me a ride home on her way to work." She couldn't resist letting her fingers enjoy the soft, still too perfect hair, just once. Then she let her gaze take the dare into the dangerous eyes. "Sleep well."

Chapter 24

Sharon answered the door, coffee cup in hand. "Morning, Dee," she greeted. "You want me to drop you off home?"

"That depends. Is Sage working today?"

"Nope. One of the perks of being the boss."

Deanne stepped out of her boots and left them at the door. "Is she up?"

"Yeah. I think I heard the crip hobbling out of the bathroom. I try not to laugh. I know it's gotta hurt like hell. But she's so damn sure of herself all the time that seeing her like this just makes me laugh."

"I know the feeling." She declined a cup of coffee. "You don't have to give me a ride. I'll see what I can do to help the crip, and take a cab."

Sharon laughed. "She'll love that. Tell her I've got her keys to the new unit, and that I'll have Kasey call her this afternoon."

"Okay."

Sage's door was slightly ajar. Deanne knocked lightly. The door swung open with the rubber end of a crutch nudging it along. Deanne peered around the corner of the dresser. Sage sat at the other end of the crutch, on the edge of the bed.

"How's my patient?"

Sage gave her a comfortable smile. "Didn't sleep much. I iced it already this morning. I was just about to wrap it."

Sleep wasn't a luxury Deanne had enjoyed either. She had been taunted all night by the alluring eyes, the gentle embrace. Would she have made the choice to come today if it weren't to return the car? She looked down at the grotesquely swollen foot resting gingerly on the arm of the chair. A dark purple-red coloring had emerged along the lower outside edge. The rest was bright pink from the ice.

"I'll wrap it for you." She draped her jacket over the other arm of the chair and picked up the neatly rerolled wrap. Quickly anchoring the end, she snugged the elastic into its familiar pattern, as efficiently as the nurse had the night before.

"Have you been moonlighting as a private nurse?"

Deanne looked up the bare leg to the gray nightshirt, buttoned only half way up. "I did so many knees and ankles when I coached that I could probably do it in my sleep."

Sharon stopped in the doorway. "If you're sure you don't need a ride Dee I'm gonna take off."

"I'm fine. Thanks Sharon."

"Have a good day, then," she said with a wink. "See you tonight."

Deanne finished the end with a piece of tape. "How's that feel?"

"As good as it can. I thought you had an interview?" Sage asked, slightly bewildered. She watched Deanne reach for the door and close it. Suddenly, she was standing directly in front of her.

"I thought you wanted to get into my pants."

Sage looked up to make eye contact. "I may have put it more delicately."

"You could have last night," she said, gliding her fingers through the soft, neat curls.

"I know."

Her eyes were distinctly green and intensely determined as they locked their gaze onto Sage's. The excitement between them was undeniable; the air around them was charged with it. It was time to acknowledge what Sage had recognized from the beginning. Deanne closed in to the edge of the bed, between Sage's legs. She leaned down and brushed her open mouth over Sage's lips. Her voice was just above a whisper. "Let's get it over with."

"God, you're romantic."

Deanne straightened without breaking eye contact. She gathered the bottom of her sweater, lifted it until she added the edge of her sports bra, and continued up and over her head. The expansion of her chest outlined her torso, rib by rib. Abdominal muscles tightened in distinct definition. Then a shift of her hips, and she quickly discarded the rest of her garments onto the end of the bed.

Eyes that had seen their fair share of naked women, now boldly made their assessment. What Sage saw made her marvel — a body tight and trim, 34B held high and firm. She allowed herself one last pass, before meeting Deanne's eyes. "You were very wrong about one thing. You're an exceptionally sexy woman."

The warmth of Sage's hands enveloped Deanne's waist, moved up her back, smoothly defined its shape, and pressed her closer. Lips, open and soft, brushed hot whispers over the waiting breasts, as a soft low moan found its way from deep in Deanne's throat. Like lightning transcending to earth, the heat traveled through her body; then centered quickly, just as it had before, merely from the glance of her eyes on her, from the smell of her perfume, from the feel of her hand.

"Are you sure this is what you want?" Sage whispered.

"I've wanted you for weeks. I can't take anymore." She closed her arms around Sage's shoulders. Closed her need around the woman who was making her break all of the rules she had used to protect herself. A breach of them, she knew, put her in almost certain emotional danger — exactly where she was now. Sage looked into her eyes, past the thin facade, uncloaked her soul, and took her breast into the heat of her mouth. Dangerously, second by second, the excitement grew.

Merely the touch of this woman thwarted Deanne's attempt at thought. Effective reasoning wasn't possible and hadn't been for some time. Her body was alive with sensation, her heart beating rapidly against her chest. Sage was doing things with her tongue and her mouth that sent wonderful sensations rippling from her breasts down through her abdomen and farther. Then in the midst of Deanne's broken thought and increasing arousal, Sage's fingers easily found the zipper of her jeans. Her hands slipped in around her hips and with polished precision slid Deanne's pants and jeans to her ankles. *Oh, yes, she had done this a few times.* Warm caresses traveled her legs, her buttocks, and up again to her back. Sage's tender lips traced the quivering contours of her abdominals, down across the shuddering flatness, and nuzzled the thick patch of brown hair. Deanne gasped with anticipation, her body responding with a rush of heat and fluid.

Sage lifted her into her arms, over her thigh, and lowered her onto the bed. Carefully, she maneuvered herself, throbbing foot in tow, alongside the woman she thought had eluded her. Deanne reached for the two remaining buttons on Sage's nightshirt, and watched Sage slip it off her shoulders. Exposed beneath was a thin white scar that ran down the large neck muscle, angled across the collarbone, and traveled downward sharply toward her breast. A strangely familiar pattern. The scar was the only blemish on Sage's otherwise smooth tan skin. Deanne gently fingered its path and started to say something. Sage met her open lips instead, kissing her deeply and thoroughly for the first time. Deanne lost her breath, breathed deeply through her nose, as the most intense sensation shot to her very core. The urgency of the open wetness of Deanne's kisses made Sage smile. She looked into Deanne's eyes ardent with desire, and tasted her quivering lips with her tongue, and abandoned her initial tenderness. Deanne met her mouth firmly, wildly. Without reservation, she coveted the full sensuous lips that had teased her for so long.

As Deanne claimed the pleasures of her mouth, Sage's smooth accomplished hands were knowing and gentle, in direct contrast to the fury of their kisses. Her hands easily found what pleased her and claiming their rights to her desire. Sage left the urgency of Deanne's mouth; ravaging the tender skin of her neck and chest with desire just short of marking her. Deanne's breathing quickened in response, her hips lifting and accepting. She gasped at the sound of her name being whispered hotly against her chest. The passion between them suddenly became personal, emotional. Exactly what she had hoped would not happen. But there was no turning back. She wanted Sage Bristo, more than she had wanted anyone in a very long time.

Deanne's hands detected the last barrier between them and slipped her hands under the waistband. "Please," she said breathlessly. "I need to feel you, all of you." Deanne slid them as far as she could, and Sage removed them gingerly. Sage slowly lowered herself on top of her lover, sliding her good leg between Deanne's.

"Ohh," Deanne sighed, as she shifted to meet Sage's long smooth body, sliding into the hot wet skin. "Ohh, yes." Her words gradually muffled into a moan as her body moved rhythmically with Sage's. Slowly and sensuously, they moved, pressing their breasts to one another, their hips, their thighs, again their breasts. Feeling and welcoming each other, they explored an intimacy their bodies demanded of them.

The tempo of their lovemaking was Deanne's. Automatically, her body sent its cues telling of her pleasure, telling of her readiness. In her need, she grasped Sage's buttocks, pulled her in, and surrendered to her. The wonderfully agonizing ache had transformed itself into a tension that increased with every movement between them. Sage moved on her with passion, yet with a touch more tender than she had ever before felt. Her mouth went again to Deanne's breasts, circling and carefully biting the erect nipples. Surges of heat shot through Deanne's body, and demanding more. Sage gave it, until the breathing turned to short gasps and Deanne's embrace tightened around her. Then Sage slipped her hand in place of her thigh and brought Deanne's pleasure to direct center.

Deanne's arousal was deeper than she'd ever imagined. Never before had a lover provided such perfect chemistry, nor coiled such excitement so tightly. Sage knew every sensitive place and touched each one perfectly. She teased her, gave to her, more than any other lover. It was as if she knew the uniqueness, the desperation, of her desire and savored its acknowledgment. Mercilessly, Sage teased through the silken folds, kissing her deeply with her tongue, until the tension reached its summit.

"We're touching the edge, aren't we?" Sage whispered. "Hold on to it," she whispered against Deanne's responding cry. "Oh, sweet baby, hold on to it."

She tried, pulling back from Sage's hand for an instant. But it was beyond control. She cried out, thrusting her hips upward, her body beginning to shutter. Sage entered in time for the powerful contractions to grasp her over and over again. Sunlight was streaming across her face as Deanne cried out the name she swore she'd never come to; cried out breathless gratitude for a most incredible orgasm. The power of it exhausted her and left her gasping for breath. Yet, her body wasn't through. With each internal stroke, sharp spasms shook her again and again, until even with decreased intensity, she could take no more. She grasped Sage's hand and stilled her while her body quivered around it. She held her there, in still rapture, until she could catch her breath.

She reached into Sage's steamy wetness to complete their lovemaking. Sage's body tensed at her touch. She removed Deanne's hand, pressed the palm of it to her lips, and took her into her arms. Deanne relaxed and softened into her embrace. In silence they held each other; not a word of love passing between them.

Sage resisted saying the words. She kept the emotion she felt for this woman to herself. For even in the depth of passion, which must have involved serious emotion, she had heard not one word of love. Although it was a rare occasion for Sage Bristo to fear speaking her mind, this was more like speaking her heart, and she wasn't ready to make herself so vulnerable. Deanne must call this hand.

Slow gentle caresses drew lightly over Sage's back and shoulders, sending a shiver through her. She kissed the delicate skin beneath Deanne's ear and whispered, "Are you going to tell me what this is all about?"

Face still tucked against Sage's shoulder, she replied, "I wanted to know what all the fuss was about."

Sage pulled back enough to force eye contact. "And?"

"Highly overrated."

Sage fell back out of their embrace, laughing. "You seduce a cripple, then rate her sexual prowess? You're a cruel woman, Deanne."

"I seduced?"

"What would you call it? A broken foot is hardly seductive."

"I merely decided to play the game using your rules."

"My rules. I don't recall indicating that I have any." She watched Deanne sit up, and reached for her arm. "You're guessing Deanne. What if you guessed wrong — at the expense of breaking one of your own rules?"

"What rule are you talking about?"

"Now I'm venturing a guess. I'm guessing that Deanne Demore has never in her life done anything like this. And further, that it breaks her rule of sleeping with someone she doesn't love."

Deanne briskly swung her legs off the bed, and grabbed Sage's nightshirt. "I have no intention of sleeping here." Donning the shirt, she abruptly left the room.

Perfectly evaded, Sage flopped back into the pillows in frustration, wincing in pain with the jarring of her swollen foot. It was beginning to throb now, without the passion to mute the pain impulses. She had begun to unwrap the aching incubus when Deanne returned.

"Here, I'll do it. Take this," she said, handing Sage a glass of water and a pain pill. Silently, she went about unwrapping and applying ice while Sage watched in wonderment.

Finally Sage asked, "Is it that hard for you to believe I could want more than your body?"

"You want a private nurse, willing to trade services for sex." A cynical smile crossed Deanne's lips as she shed the nightshirt and began dressing. "I only ask one thing of you . . . that you keep what happened between us to yourself."

"I will, but I'm not buying this unemotional facade I don't believe you're made that way. Not after what we just experienced."

Deanne pulled her sweater over her head and swept her fingers through her hair, lifting it to let it fall casually in place. "As insightful as those words probably are, they seem to lose something coming from a naked woman with her foot propped in the air." She held the nightshirt out teasingly, and when Sage reached for it, she pulled it back. "Hmm, your vulnerability is actually quite appealing."

"Is that so?" Sage leaned back on her elbows. "Then come here," she said with a look in her eyes that sent an electrical current shooting through Deanne.

"My cab will be here any minute." She pulled her eyes

away, and dropped the nightshirt in Sage's lap. "Besides, you can't hurt what you don't have."

"You're that sure I would?" Deanne turned to leave. "And if you're wrong?"

Deanne looked briefly into her eyes, then turned and left.

Chapter 25

Card night was difficult. It ran a close second to facing Angie and her friends for the first time after the breakup. There were plenty of excuses, ready and believable, for skipping it. Still, she had to face Sage sooner or later, and later always had a way of magnifying the anxiety. So here she was, dodging the searching brown eyes, wrestling torturous feelings of desire, and fast-talking her heart into behaving itself.

In the dim hallway Deanne finally found some relief. *Maybe the bathroom was empty, and she could stand there the rest of the evening, waiting for nobody to come out. Sure, and that would probably qualify as some sort of infantile avoidance complex.* She was forced to face the music when the bathroom door opened suddenly. Sage took her by the arm and pulled her in.

"Sage, don't do this," she protested, while allowing herself to be pulled into an embrace.

"Don't prove you wrong? Don't tell you I've been trying to call you all week? That I want more than sex from you?" She kissed the side of her head and felt Deanne's arms circle her waist.

"This is one time in my life when I desperately want to be wrong, Sage. But the more I'm around you, the more complicated my life becomes. I find myself making decisions that scare the hell out of me."

"Right or wrong, Deanne, you were with me all week. In my car, in my office, at every meeting. Every time I relaxed for even a minute, there you were. My life isn't as simple as it once was."

Deanne nestled into their mutual embrace. "Would it be easier if I were younger?"

"I doubt it. I think this has more to do with trust than it does with age."

Sage was right, of course. She wouldn't believe her if she were 33 any more than she does now. Maybe she would have been a little more willing to chance a short fling then, but would have been no more trusting of their values being compatible. Besides, who was she trying to fool? She couldn't fool herself anymore; and she certainly wasn't fooling Sage. She wanted this to continue. Deanne wanted Sage, wanted her arms around her, wanted her to do all the things to her again that drove her wildly to ecstasy. They both knew it. She pressed a kiss into Sage's neck, breathing in her exciting scent.

"What is it you wear?" she whispered. "I've looked everywhere."

"So, it's Observ'e L' Essence that finally gets you into my arms."

"Mmm, absolutely. Without it, all this attractiveness, this commanding presence of yours . . ." She looked up into seductive eyes. "The way you look at me, the way you touch me . . . would have no effect at all."

The touch of her hand on her face and the look in Sage's eyes stripped away all that remained of Deanne's resistance. The words were whispered puffs across her face. "Then I must protect my French connection with my life."

Deanne lifted her mouth to the soft warm lips, conceded to wanting them, yielded to their immediate passion. After all her resistance and self-admonition, she was giving in once again to the woman she feared would never commit to her, and in the secrecy of a bathroom, no less. What was even more frightening was the possibility that she was in love with her. *Wasn't it enough she hadn't yet admitted to herself that it was only at cards she could qualify as a player? How could a commitment-oriented, emotionally vulnerable woman ever expect to play the game of sexual hardball? Never mind that it was with Dr. Feelgood. Where was Jackie Madouse when she needed her to inject a little virtual reality into her senses?*

None of that mattered at this point. Deanne's body, now steeped with desire, was enjoying the feel of Sage's body pressing into hers. Their kisses, searching deep for unbridled passion, made her forget where she was; and for now, forget the consequences as well. She ignored everything, except what Sage Bristo was doing to her body, until they heard reality entering the front door. Sage groaned as Deanne withdrew her lips.

Although her breathing was far from normal, and all visible skin was flushed with excitement, Deanne cleared her throat and said quietly. "They're back with the food. I'd better go down with them."

Sage cupped the flushed face in her hands and spoke softly. "You're going to be quite uncomfortable, unless I finish what I started."

A painful sigh freed itself from Deanne's chest. "Please, don't make this harder than it is."

"If you're worried about making too much noise, we'll go somewhere else."

"I told you, I don't want the others to know."

Sage loosened her embrace and stared thoughtfully at the woman in her arms. "You know, Deanne, I have feelings, too. What particular feeling do you think is evoked by the fact that you'll sleep with me but not date me?" Deanne made no reply, looking somewhere in the vicinity of Sage's belt. "You're embarrassed to have slept with me."

"Being a statistic would be embarrassing," she said finally. "I've already played the fool in my life. I've been the last to know. I've tried to make the impossible work. I'm not being a fool about this. When you hurt me, I want to deal with it privately."

"I will never intentionally hurt you, Deanne. There's a lot of emotion involved in what's going on between us, and I'll admit I'm not real familiar with it. But the last thing I want to do is hurt you."

"Hurt is hurt, intentional or not. If I am to get to the point where I can trust how I feel and trust how you feel, it's going to take time. I'm asking for that time to be private."

"I already promised you that," she said with a gentle kiss.

"Okay." She slipped from their embrace. "I'll see you downstairs."

"Anyone interested in ordering pictures from the wedding, fill out a form so Deanne can take them with her tonight," announced Kasey, placing the preview book in the middle of the table.

Laura turned the pages, with Jan and Ali looking over her shoulder. "These are beautiful, Deanne."

"Thank you, but I had some pretty terrific looking subjects. That always makes me look good."

"Don't be modest," Kasey said, briefly massaging her shoulders. "You're good."

"Wow, Sage!" exclaimed Laura. "Who is the black woman you were with at the wedding?"

"Is she a model or something?" asked Jan.

"She's a friend from New York." She said the words as if they held no importance, yet her tone lacked commitment. "She used to model. She's a buyer for Saks, now."

The French connection deciphered Deanne. *Protect it with your life.*

"Well, excuse me," grinned Jan. "But there's enough steam rising from these pictures to curl my toes and straighten my hair."

Brown eyes stared coldly across the table. "Just a friend, Jan."

An expressionless Deanne rose from her seat, moved to the other side of the room, and retrieved her glass.

Sharon reappeared from the direction of the laundry room, her mouth twisted into a cocky smirk. "Yeah. That 'friend' left behind black lace. These," she held up a pair of red jockey bikinis — "must be yours Deanne."

An immediate blush of red and obvious shock registered on Deanne's face. In a fury, she closed the distance to Sharon, grabbed the panties, and threw them forcefully in Sage's face. She spun about, and with fierce determination, headed for the stairs. While the others watched in stunned silence, Sage limped her pursuit in unmistakable pain. Unable to catch her, she stopped at the base of the stairway and called. "Deanne! Wait."

"Don't follow me! Don't call me!" Deanne's voice echoed down the stairway, followed by the resounding slam of the front door.

Sage braced her hands between the stairway walls and momentarily hung her head. No one said a word. She turned slowly, eyes of ice freezing Sharon in mid-thought. The air still stung with Deanne's anguish, while Sharon struggled awkwardly for a way to temper the increasing antipathy.

"I didn't mean for it to —"

"I'll be back tomorrow for the rest of my things." She disappeared up the stairs before anyone else spoke.

Finally, Jan offered, "Houston, we have a problem."

"I'll say," agreed Laura.

"No one can say I didn't warn her," remarked Ali flippantly.

"Why, Sharon?" Kasey asked. "Why can't you stop and think about other people's feelings when you're tempted to do something so stupid?"

"I didn't mean to hurt Deanne. I just get so pissed at Sage. She has to be so goddamn secretive about who she's screwin'."

"Some would see that as a virtue," replied Connie with noticeable chastisement.

Laura stood decisively. "All right. Someone has to talk to Sage, other than Sharon. And you," she turned to face Sharon, "need to call Deanne."

"Sage." Kasey addressed her through the slightly ajar door. "Can I talk to you?"

Sage was uncharacteristically throwing things into a bag, limping between the dresser and the bed. "There's nothing to talk about."

"I brought your crutches up."

"Thanks." She zipped the bag and reached for the crutches.

Kasey didn't let go of them until Sage made eye contact. "You're in love with her, aren't you?"

"It doesn't matter."

"I think it does. That's why you're reacting like this. Knowing you both as well as I do puts me in a unique position. I hope you'll take advantage of that and listen to me."

Sage started past her, and knowing better than to try to stop her, Kasey took the bag and walked with her to the car. "Deanne's a lot like me, Sage. That's why I can say this with conviction. She's too sensitive for her own good at times. The same things that you've been able to harden yourself against upset her. She has no idea what to do with you except to love you. And she's too consumed in her own pain right now to recognize yours."

"Then you know Deanne well enough to know that she's just been given the last reason she needs never to talk to me again."

"Give her a little time. But you can't be afraid to tell her you love her. I thank God Connie was aggressive enough to tell me. Lord knows how badly you and I might have messed each other up." Kasey noticed an acknowledgment, however slight, in Sage's eyes. "If it's meant to be, Sage, love has a way of overcoming whatever is put in its path. I tell you from experience — it is the single most powerful emotion."

She threw the crutches into the backseat. "If this is how loves makes you feel, I have no use for it."

Chapter 26

Deanne stared at the opened envelope, with its typed address, lying in the middle of the table. Clever, she had to admit. Sharon must have guessed the handwritten ones had been burned without being opened. This one at least survived that fate. The signature at the bottom, though, was all she'd needed to see. She tossed Sharon's letter back onto the table unread. If she refused to read Sage's, why should she honor Sharon's? She'd perform the ceremonial burning later.

She had told Jodie nothing, despite her uncanny ability to sense her every mood, even over the phone. Jodie knew. It wasn't necessary to inflict more pain, with an account of sleeping with Sage, or even grant some probably deserved satisfaction of knowing she had been right. Once again, a woman chosen over her had not been able to equal the love she offered. In all actuality, Deanne figured, she and Jodie were destined for each another. Life, she was beginning to see, was like that. You take care of each another and love the best way you can. And you make your dreams into stories.

She wondered back into the kitchen. For a long moment she stared into the refrigerator, then closed the door without taking anything out. She filled a glass with cold water and found herself setting it down next to the letter. "No. Dammit! I don't need your pathetic apology, and I will not relieve your piss-poor excuse for a conscience," she said aloud. She wadded the paper tightly into a ball and banked it off the kitchen wall to land where she couldn't see it. "Live with it."

Why should it concern her how they feel? Her feelings obviously didn't matter. What was she to them, anyway? A steady player every other Thursday night and a challenge met and conquered. That's all. End of story.

The phone rang. Deanne flopped onto the couch and opened her signed copy of Urvashi Vaid's *Virtual Equality*. The answering machine clicked on and the caller hung up. They had stopped leaving messages last week. Kasey's had been the only one returned. Unwilling to speak for anyone else, she had urged Deanne to speak directly to Sage and Sharon. That, Deanne vowed, was not going to happen not for a long, long time.

The paragraph, reread for the third time, wasn't making a connection. She turned back a page. Hadn't she read this? She turned back another page. *Shit! When did the words stop registering?* She tossed the book down on the end of the couch. *Sorry, Urvashi, I'm afraid Jackie Madouse would be more appropriate company right now.* She needed a piece of ground-level advice and work-boot logic that only the ever-candid Jackie could offer. Deanne clicked into Windows, and opened Jackie's file. She scanned to a blank page and let her talk.

"So, she got you in bed. Big fucking deal. And she bragged

about it. Hey, there musta been somethin' there to brag about. Right? What's that say? Forty-three-year-old-woman, hot enough to get the almighty Sage Bristo chasing her. Pretty damn good, I'd say. Makes my nips hard just thinkin' about it. Jesus to Jenny, girl, do a little braggin' of your own."

Good one, Jackie, she laughed to herself. The quintessential philosopher always made her feel better. If she had only a smidgen of Jackie's egotism, Deanne Demore would be published by now — and surely more capable of handling an affair with Sage Bristo. But her re-emerging sense of trust had taken a direct hit. Her fragile self-confidence had faced its first real test and had taken a definitive nosedive.

Clearly, if she refused the phone calls and never read the letters, she could continue to be mad or hurt or whatever it was that was making it easier to deal with the situation. That would be easier, but admittedly not the most mature approach. Was that the reason she was here, in the kitchen, looking everywhere for a damn wadded up piece of paper? Probably. It was time to grow up, learn from life, instead of trying to make it into some idealistic abstraction of the real thing. *Something Jackie's been trying to tell me for years.* Or was the real reason for her sudden flurry of anxiety the haunting words of Sage Bristo, "What if you're wrong?" What price might she already have paid?

She was still looking for the letter's final resting place. She couldn't have hidden it any better if she'd tried. *Oh, sure, double-bank it blind off the wall and the cupboard, and sink it right into the leftover SpaghettiOs. And you stopped playing basketball.* She smoothed the wrinkled paper over a paper towel, and finally read:

Dear Deanne,

You aren't the only one not speaking to me. Sage moved out the same night. She hasn't returned my calls, either. Kasey took me off the job at Longhouse and put me on another, at Sage's request. But, that's not why I'm sorry for what I did.

I didn't realize how much what I did hurt you and your relationship with Sage. I was selfish and thoughtless. I'm sorry Deanne.

Sage has never said one word to me, or anyone else that I know of, about a personal relationship with you. That's one thing that's always frustrated me about Sage. She never tells me anything about her personal life. It was my own selfish interest that hurt you both.

I don't know if you can ever forgive me. I don't think Sage ever will. I've always teased her, mercilessly at times. But, she has never reacted like this. There must be a lot more involved than I understand. I'm sorry, Deanne. Please don't judge Sage for what I've done.

Sharon

"I'm sorry," said the voice on the other end. "Ms. Bristo left hours ago."

"Look, this is very important. Is there another number where she can be reached?"

"I'm not at liberty to give out that information. Ms. Bristo will be in New York until next week. I can have her call you when she returns."

"No, that's all right. Thank you."

Deanne hung up; she hesitated only seconds before dialing the next number. "Sharon, this is Deanne." Without allowing her time to respond, she continued, "I'm not ready to talk to you. All I want is some phone numbers. Sage may have already left for New York, I don't know. Just give me some numbers, here or there, where I might reach her tonight."

"Try her sister first," she replied. "But if she's still

here — it's Wednesday — I'll give you the address." Deanne scratched the numbers on an envelope. "Deanne, you should go over and introduce yourself, even if Sage has left."

Trusting Sharon felt a lot like trusting the IRS to figure your taxes, but the sight of the Explorer in the driveway made her forget all about Sharon. She tried concentrating on a mature, unemotional apology, a task made even harder by not knowing whom she was about to meet — a model-type in black lace, a tall blond athlete, a friend, or a lover. Ready or not, these were questions about to be answered, and maybe a few others. For this was a test Deanne needed to pass, as uncomfortable as it was. She was well aware that Sage Bristo may no longer be interested in her or her apology.

With a deep breath Deanne knocked at the door. When it opened, at least two important questions were answered immediately. Greeting her was a small pixie of a woman with a strawberry blond bob and an impish smile that made pinpointing her age over sixty impossible.

"Hello. My name is Deanne. I'm a friend of Sage's."

The blue-gray eyes twinkled happily. "Come in, dear, come in. I'm afraid she hasn't much time, though. She has to catch a plane. Her sister's getting married Friday." Her face was animated with excitement. "I've never seen her so nervous."

"Esther, I —" Sage stopped at the sight of Deanne, but recovered quickly. "Deanne Demore, this is Esther Yeager. Your timing, Ms. Demore, is terrible."

"Let me drive you to the airport. I'd like to talk to you before you leave."

"The car will be fine in the driveway," Esther assured her. "You'd better scoot, dear. You don't want to miss your plane."

Sage placed the keys on the table. "No doughnuts in the parking lot." She leaned over, hugged the little woman with obvious affection, and kissed her cheek. "I'll see you when I get back."

"Safe journey."

"It was very nice to meet you," Deanne smiled.

"Wednesday nights," grinned Deanne, her eyes on the road.

"You're surprised."

"Pleased."

"I met her over a year ago. She was trying to drag a fallen branch three times her size from her driveway. It was love at first sight."

"Surrogate grandmother?"

"Maybe." Sage shifted in her seat to lean her back against the door. "Whose letter did you finally read?"

"The last one Sharon sent. She typed it. No return address."

"You realize we underestimated her."

"Obviously. And just as obviously, I owe you a huge apology. We've been doing this since the beginning it seems. I'm sorry, Sage."

"Apologize only for jumping to a conclusion, not for your emotional pain. That's something I understand quite well. I only handle it differently. Are you going to let me in on where it comes from? Or do you enjoy watching me guess my way through this?"

"Through what?"

"This thing we have between us."

"I never realized," Deanne said quietly. "I'll bore you with it sometime, if you're really interested." She was aware of Sage staring at her. She kept her eyes safely ahead. "There are a few things I'd like to know, too."

"Ask them."

"Okay. To start, how did Sharon know what kind of under-wear I wear?"

"That I honestly don't know. Now that I think about it, they came off so fast, I didn't know myself."

"Oh!"

Sage intercepted Deanne's fist about to strike her leg. She laughed as she unfolded it into her own.

"Okay, dammit. Are you ready for the tough questions?"

"How tough can they be?"

"Who's the woman in the restaurant?"

"Don't know. Never saw her before. I have dated enough of her kind, though, to know what she was all about."

"Did you sleep with Ali?"

"This is really important to you. No, little Dee Berry, I did not."

"Dee Berry? I swear that man will tell every secret I have."

"He's told me more about you than you have."

The smile that greeted her was the very one that greeted her that first card night. Sweet and sincere, it made her feel as if she were the only one in the world ever to receive it. She hated to ask the next question and risk it being taken from her.

"Is that as tough as they get?"

"I'm afraid not. How close a friend is the woman in the wedding pictures?"

As expected, Sage's smile disappeared into a resolute pensiveness. "A longtime friend . . . and lover. Our relationship has never been monogamous, and our only commitment has been to friendship."

"Why?"

"We want different things out of life. Tia has an apartment in New York that she visits about once a month and a handsome dyke in every major city. What makes me special to her is that she can always count on my friendship. That part hasn't changed. But I haven't slept with anyone since I met you. Can you say the same?"

"No," she said, almost inaudibly. "I can't." She was sufficiently embarrassed at her own hypocrisy. Sage politely let the subject drop. Deanne concentrated on traffic. Finally, she asked, "What does Sage want from life?"

"And need? A sense of home. A place where I feel safe and loved. I don't know if that's possible. Sharon's home has been the closest thing to it since my grandmother died."

"Before I met Cimmie, I never would have believed that about you. You don't make it easy for people to get to know you."

"Another form of protection. The effort becomes important in itself. If someone cares enough to stick around that long, they at least end up with a good friend. I don't trust easily, either."

The area was becoming increasingly more congested as they neared the terminal. Sage released Deanne's hand and began organizing papers and making notes in her Franklin. "Come with me to New York," she said suddenly.

"Sage, why do you do this to me? I can't drop everything and run to New York with you." She pulled in as close as possible, double-parking in front of the Northwest sign.

"Why not? Park the car. I'll pay for parking and get you a ticket right now."

Deanne opened the trunk and pulled out Sage's bags. "I'm not like you, Sage. I can't make decisions like you do." She carried the black leather garment bag to the porter's stand and began backing toward the car.

"Take a chance for once in your life. Come with me."

Deanne shook her head. "Safe trip."

"What's stopping you?"

"My job. Assignments." She started to turn away, then added, "I don't know what you want from me."

"I want the truth about how you feel."

Someone honked. Deanne looked irritated as she opened the car door.

"Tell me, Deanne," Sage shouted over the commotion.

"Stop it, Sage." Deanne's voice rose sharply over the roof of the car. "You're embarrassing me."

"Tell me."

"Tell you what?" She shouted back. "That I want you, that I need you?" She was ignoring the honking now, and the stares.

"No. Something I don't know."

Tears formed in her eyes as she shouted. "That I love you?"

"Yes! Do you?"

"Yes. I love you," she shouted, before dropping hurriedly into the seat, and pulling aggressively into traffic.

She sped down Interstate 94, unaware of the traffic, maneuvering by rote, at a speed ten miles over the limit. The adrenaline still coursing through her body had lost its purpose. It served only as nervous energy now. Deanne clutched the wheel tightly and sat forward in her seat to scan the radio stations. Yet despite her best efforts at distraction, the shouting match continued to replay itself, over and over. She found no relief for having made the admission, a confession forced from her. *In front of all those people!*

The car slowed to a respectable speed in the right lane. Deanne leaned back against the seat and dropped her hands to the bottom of the steering wheel. *Such a spectacle, for no one except Sage Bristo.* She smiled at what expressions she must have missed. *Scary, love's power. Downright scary.*

It wasn't until she stopped the car in the driveway that Deanne saw the envelope with her name on it, tucked next to the seat. Inside the fancy invitation to Cimmie's wedding were five hundred dollars and a single slip of paper. Written in Sage's distinctive longhand were three words: I love you.

Chapter 27

"No! No!" The words that startled her awake left Deanne shaking and frightened. Her own voice, her own words, yelled from the depths of another world. A world as familiar as her bedroom but unable to be totally recalled. Her T-shirt was soaked with perspiration, causing her to shiver in the cool night air. She pulled the old quilt back over her shoulders, closed her eyes, and tried to bring back the visions.

Flashes of a figure taunted her mind, darting behind closed eyes, daring her mind to recognize it. She reached for the light next to the bed and her pad and pencil. Frantically, she wrote the descriptive words of the sketchy vision before it was gone: *Atop a wooded hill — face to the sky — long dark waves — arms raised to her sides.*

The dream from so long ago. Suddenly the concept was there, with glimpses only an instant long flashing quickly through her mind. Yes, she was remembering. That's where they were coming from all this time. She grabbed her robe, swung open the closet door, and pulled all the boxes from the shelf. Like a woman possessed, she sat on the floor, searching through box after box, folder after folder, until she found it. In a collection of early writings, handwritten on yellow legal paper, the words brought back the visions of twenty years ago.

The Dream

It begins as it always does, with a sense of hushed stillness. My sleep becomes anxious, for I know I will see her. She always appears first as a distant figure on the hill. My mind circles overhead. Closer. Until I can feel her intensity. The darkened figure kneels, and I know she is intently keeping watch.

I feel the cool night air tingling against my face. It is still and calm and smells thickly of pine. She feels the night differently than I. Her ears are finely tuned to the song of the wind, trained to hear any interruption in its melody. Her eyes carefully watch a nearby doe and her fawn, eating in the safety of darkness. She observes not for pleasure, but to use the doe's keener senses as an alarm. I watch with her, waiting for what quickens her heart. Perfectly still.

The large ears of the doe turn back once. We hold our breath and listen. Twice. The doe's head jerks upward into frozen alert. In the space of an instant, she is gone. The kneeling woman rises, heart beating rapidly with my own. She breathes the air deeply, sensing something that sends her swiftly down the hill.

Her urgency makes me anxious. My heart races with her to the long crude structures below. From one to the next, she runs, five in all. Women and children flow silently from each, disappearing into the woods. Danger looms in the air, creeping like a heavy fog, ever closer.

Men hurry to positions at the base of the hill. The woman emerges from the shadows. I can see her now, momentarily visible in the moonlight, tall and strong in movement, naked to the waist. A distinctive white marking, illuminated by the moon, stretches like a jagged streak of lightning from the right side of her neck to her chest. She will join the men now. Like them, she is a warrior.

In utter stillness I wait with them, trying to control my heavy breathing. And then they came, darkened forms creeping toward the houses and their sleeping prey. I sense the warrior's fear as it transcends space and time. Nearly out of control, its chill fills me. But she has seen battle before, and pulls her fear within, to an undetectable place.

All at once, there is a rush of movement, and the enemy is surrounded. Warriors wield their weapons with fierce determination. Blow after deadly blow, the woman warrior delivers, blocking enemy strikes with a small crude shield. Powerfully, she swings her weapon, showing no signs of weariness. Somehow I understand. She will fight to her death if needed, for she dare not be captured alive.

Blood is everywhere. The sounds of dying all around. The warrior fighting back to back with her falls against her leg. She straddles his body protectively, wields her weapon for two now. She strikes rapidly to the right, and to the left. Fearlessly, she faces enemy after enemy, fighting on, past exhaustion.

When suddenly from behind, an enemy approaches with his weapon poised to strike. Fear freezes my very blood from flowing. I must warn her, but no sound

comes from my throat. My mind hurriedly tries to open the vise of fear, to shout, but, the bloodcurdling scream is not my own. It is the enemy about to strike. I cannot bear it. My mind tumbles and runs from the sight. I wouldn't be able to bear her pain or bear to lose her. I run with my mind, faster and harder. Tears stream down my face. Screams fill my ears. I cannot tell if they are hers or my own. I am more afraid to think they are hers, and I realize, I cannot leave her. Terrified and exhausted, I run back. I hear the sounds from my throat.
"No! No!"

She sat in stunned revelation. The mystery unmasking itself before her was too incredible for even Deanne to believe. She stared at the drawing she'd made of the marking on the warrior's neck and chest. Twenty years ago, she'd planned to research its origin. She never could have guessed its significance.

Chapter 28

Deanne's cab trip from the airport to the church could have qualified for a Spielberg movie. Her concept of driving had undergone a drastic reeducation: brakes were to be applied only to keep from actually hitting the vehicle in front of you; the horn was the most important part of the car, to be used in place of the brakes; and an open space belonged to the driver with the quickest reactions and the least amount of concern for bodily damage. She arrived at the church wishing she had taken a double dose of Dramamine.

Over three hundred guests filled the pews and witnessed the beautifully orchestrated ceremony. Deanne couldn't be sure Sage even knew she was there. The grand old church, vaulted and elaborately ornate, was the perfect setting for a ceremony steeped in elegant tradition. Cimmie, of course, was predictably gorgeous with silk and lace, and tasteful cleavage. Her groom glowed with pride in black and white. But, Sage was magnificent. Long sleek lines of dark satin wine, shimmered in ambient light. It was doubtful that her Hassey could even do her justice, although, she'd have sacrificed three assignments to try.

The crowd was slowly migrating toward the huge wooden doors. Deanne clutched her overnight bag and joined the throng, nudging and smiling her way along. Just as a right or left decision became necessary, an arm slipped around her waist. Sage's voice was against her ear. "Following the yellow-brick road?"

"Yes," Deanne smiled. "So far, it's managed to scare the hell out of me."

"Follow me, Dorothy," she laughed. "There's a lot to see before you go home."

The minimal participation by John Capra in his daughter's wedding may have gone unnoticed by most. Cimmie's choice to walk the aisle alone was the most obvious evidence thus far. But his state of ambivalence was about to be made crystal clear.

Cimmie's voice over the microphone quieted the crowd. "Traditionally, this is the time when the bride dances with that person in her life who has been her protector, the one who through the years she could always count on when she was frightened or unsure. In the twenty-nine years of my life, that person has been my sister, Sage. I've not even dared to think what my life would have been without her strength. Even when we were separated, she enrolled in all my dance classes, so that we could be together. I knew it was for me she did it. Dancing did not exactly sugar her tea at age twelve." She smiled along with the quiet laughter. "All those lessons gave me precious time to talk with my best friend. Soul-saving discussions in three-quarter time." She smiled. "Time to draw from her strength." John and Lena Capra were noticeably absent; Jeremy Capra was too drunk to care. "Even at such a young age, I recognized how much she loved me. Of course, those same lessons, made Sage into such a fine dancer that I had to begin competing with the other girls in the class to dance with her."

Cimmie watched Sage emerge through the crowd gathering around the dance floor. She dabbed her eyes with a readied tissue. "I love you Sage. I know you'll remember this; it was our favorite Viennese waltz. "

Deanne wiped tears from her own eyes and watched the sisters meet in an elegant pose in the middle of the floor. Cimmie's hand rested atop Sage's precisely angled arm, and they began their dance with classic ease. Music and movements aligned perfectly in an exquisite flow of gallantry and grace. Their bodies, a fluid interpretation of notes and emotion, swept effortlessly over the floor. They were a vision of royalty not of our time. There was no break in continuity of motion or gaze. They were perfect unity.

Watching them, realizing the uniqueness of the bond between them, brought new concerns to the surface of Deanne's mind. Would such a love outmatch the depth of any other? It would surely be the model by which all others were judged. Its impact on any relationship with Sage would only be a guess. Chances were that hoping for a love that deep, that lasting, might be nothing more than a spiteful trick of the heart. The risk was greater than any in her life, and the possible reward greater than she had ever imagined.

All she ever wanted was for her love to be enough for someone, and for a woman to love her in return, enough to make a monogamous relationship work. She believed, maybe naively, that someday that would be possible. She never asked that it be with someone like Sage Bristo. She never hoped for the kind of excitement just being near her created. She certainly never believed that a woman like Sage would want the same thing. Yet, clearly now, she was willing to take the chance to find out, no matter what the risk.

"Keep an eye on Brandon, the guy with the mustache in the gray suit," warned Cimmie in the last stanza of their waltz. "He's about to break his zipper over Deanne, and I don't want her to feel uncomfortable."

"I've been watching."

A gracious curtsy accompanied Sage's bowed head. Their classical performance ended to thunderous applause. The sisters embraced in an emotional display meant only for each other. "You'll always be my heroine," Cimmie said softly, tears streaking her cheeks.

"Are you trying to make me cry?"

"Uh-huh. I love you."

"And I love you." Sage gently kissed Cimmie's cheek. "Be happy."

"I will," Cimmie smiled, wiping a tear from Sage's face with her thumb. "Now go rescue your lady."

Curious eyes followed the sure strides of the woman in wine as she approached the table where Brandon hovered vulturously over Deanne. His preoccupation prevented him from noticing Sage until she leaned down and whispered in Deanne's ear. "I've come to rescue you." The smile that met her radiated gratitude for not having to ask.

"Hi," Deanne welcomed warmly, offering the empty chair next to her. "Sage, have you met Brandon? He works with Jeff."

Her eyes, direct and cool, met his. "Nice to meet you." Sage extended her hand, as she drew her left arm deliberately around Deanne's shoulders. His eyes zeroed in predictably on the slender fingers intentionally caressing Deanne's shoulder. His handshake was firm and abrupt.

His eyes met Deanne's. "Is this how it is?"

Deanne smiled, more at herself than Brandon. "Yes. This is how it is."

"Pretty adventuresome for a small town girl." His eyes shifted to Sage's icy stare. "The big city sure offers its share of interesting experiences." He came quickly back to Deanne's less ominous eyes, then reached into his breast pocket and handed her his card. "If you give me a call before you leave, I'm sure the three of us could produce some very interesting experiences, if you're looking for excitement."

Deanne ran her hand slowly over Sage's satin-covered thigh. "I think I have all the excitement I can handle." He turned abruptly from Deanne's smile, and disappeared among the tables.

"Why Dorothy. Are you suggesting —"

"I'm suggesting that if you don't stop looking at me like that, we are not going to make it to wherever we're going tonight."

"Is that right?"

"Ever done it in a church bathroom?"

"Uh-huh."

"Why did I ask?"

Slowly, throughout the evening, tension had coiled itself gently between them. No more obstacles of indecision impeded it; no barriers of the mind hampered their enjoyment of it. The excitement they felt now was pure. It was untainted by fear and void of anxiety. They were ready for each other.

* * * * *

The door of Cimmie's apartment closed behind them, surrounding them with long awaited privacy. They shared a heated embrace that was filled with mutual passion. Their lips tenderly expressed desire, touching with the attentiveness born of deep understanding, opening to each other in undenied yearning.

"I know what you're telling me," Deanne whispered against the soft lips. "But I need to hear you say it."

Sage gathered Deanne tighter in her arms and touched her lips tenderly to her cheek. "I love you." She kissed the delicate skin below her ear. "I love you." And the sensitive hollow of her neck. "I love you."

The words traveled through Deanne like a current, and escaped softly in a moan that made Sage smile. Her hands grasped Sage's shoulders and spread through her soft curls. "I have never fought so hard" — she said as Sage spread her hands over her buttocks, and pulled her tightly to her pelvis — "Mmm . . . Against something I want so much."

They lay naked beneath the airy warmth of the down comforter. Their caresses were warm and exciting, their kisses long and deep. The way they touched each other bore witness to their long emotional journey. They yielded softness to each other, surrendering to the honesty of their emotions.

The room, dimly lighted from the perimeter, sculpted Sage's face with soft ambiance and shadow. She slid the comforter from her shoulders and spoke in soft tones. "Let me see again how beautiful you are."

Deanne's heart quickened, transfused with the radiant heat of Sage's gaze washing over her naked body. "Those eyes made love to me, long before your hands ever did. There is no resistance left in me, only love, and desire for you." She cupped the noble face in her hand, drank from the eyes that warmed her. "It's all I have. I hope it will be enough."

"It's all I've ever wanted."

Sage's hands, long and smooth, moved delicately over Deanne's body. The desire they commanded spread with them, over her shoulders, over her breasts. Everywhere they touched, they spread heat over the bareness. Down the shapely curves of her legs and up the inside of her thighs, they moved so slowly. They knew everywhere to touch, where to linger, where to tease. The pleasure they brought was evident in Deanne's excited breath and sighs. All the while Sage's hands caressed, her eyes did likewise, coming back often to bathe in soft blue-green desire. Deanne's body became fluid motion beneath Sage's hands, rippling and lifting to meet them, expanding to fill them. Desire turned quickly to need.

In a moment when their eyes met again, Sage saw in her eyes what Deanne's body was beginning to tell her. The time was not long for such tenderness. She gathered Deanne to her, covered her with the length of her body. Deanne caught her breath, wrapped her arms and legs around the slender body. The sound she made, low and breathy, was one of passion nearing the bounds of its constraints. She laced her fingers into Sage's hair and brought their open lips together in a kiss that exploded with emotion. Each successive kiss merged the lovers deeper into one passion, one single goal. Pleasure gave way to an aching pain, which had already begun its ascent toward splendid relief. Bodies, molded in fluid heat, moved urgently now, in perfect unison. Moisture seeped from every pore. With control slipping as quickly as her lover's breath, Sage's mouth went to Deanne's body.

"Oh, God, I want you!" Deanne gasped.

"You have me, Deanne." Her breath hot was against her neck. "You have me."

Deanne quivered under searing lips that tasted the sensitive skin across her chest and beneath her breasts. Her senses, piqued, responded to the scent of her lover, the feel of her body, the sweet taste of her mouth, the sounds of her love-making. Deanne wanted Sage with every breath she breathed. Every cell of her body cried out for her touch. Her body arched upward, her breast enveloped in the heat of Sage's mouth. Sensation after sensation shot through her from swirls of her tongue over hardened nipples, from teeth expertly squeezing pleasure to its limit.

"Oh, Sage . . . ohh, yes."

"My beautiful lover," Sage murmured, slipping her arms around Deanne's arching body, moving her mouth down the tight contour between her ribs. She pressed herself into the warm wetness she knew was of her making. A moan from deep within Deanne's throat filled the air with anticipation. The same anticipation that surged the blood through Sage's veins moved her in sensuous rhythm. Their bodies were one in a consummate flow of motion. Perfect unanimity. There would be no attempt this time to slow the pace. She would give it all now, take her as quickly as she needed. From primal depth to climactic summit. For she knew she would take her there again and again.

Deanne's voice was low, husky with need. "Sage, please . . ."

Sage gave of her mouth to her lover, offered the whole of it, with all the emotion welling within her. Engulfed in liquid velvet, she caressed her lover's need to uncontrolled heights, tempered her tension to a suspended quiver.

In the fragile moment before ecstasy, Deanne felt only one desperate need. She sought only one exquisite stroke. And when it came, unleashing the final bond, her body exploded in glorious, resounding orgasm. Amid cries of exultation, her responsive hips drove upward again and again as the impulses kept coming. Then, finally she collapsed in complete exhaustion.

She reached for Sage, held her face against the heartbeat still pounding. She closed her legs tighter, stilling the fingers within. While Sage lay spent in her embrace, she drew deep breaths of blessed contentment. From her lover's lips came soft sounds, in a language Deanne did not understand. She knew only the emotion of it, like her own, tumbling forth in words of love.

Sage stirred, came to Deanne's side, and took her once again in her arms.

"What did you say, in your tongue? What did you tell me?"

"That you are the flower of my heart, the keeper of my soul."

The words caught her breath. "Have you ever —"

"Never to anyone else."

Moved to tears, Deanne traced Sage's noble features tenderly with her fingertips. She was lost irretrievably in the deepest love of her life. A love so sublime, she would go without food or sleep; so vital, she would go without life-sustaining breath, for it was life itself. "I didn't know it was possible to love someone this much." Her lips, with equal tenderness, followed her fingertips, touching lightly over Sage's face. They brushed across the proud brow, inhaling the fragrance of her hair. Her lips stopped briefly on the delicate eyelid, teased long dark lashes, explored the shape of her nose, then kissed gently over the finely sculptured cheek. She came to the wonderful lips and traced their shape with the tip of her tongue, teasing the softness with her own. They parted, and teased back with a moist heat that whetted her recovering desire. She murmured inarticulately, slipping along the length of Sage's body, becoming lissome against her. Sage lay back into the pillows. Deanne snuggled against her neck. Her voice was soft and still husky. "You take my breath away. You have from the moment I first saw you."

Sage's fingers were caressing through her hair; she pressed her lips into Deanne's hair and whispered softly. "And your smile drops me to my knees." Deanne looked up into her eyes with surprised pleasure and smiled. "You didn't know I was falling apart right before your eyes, did you?"

"No." She lifted herself to look directly into her eyes. "I

didn't, but I guarantee I'll know when you fall apart beneath me." She kissed her deeply, sensuously, before enveloping Sage's body with a full caress of her own. Sage shifted beneath her, brought her hands warmly over her back, suggestively over her buttocks. Her arms tightened around her. Renewed passion burst forth from the taste of her mouth. Again, Deanne felt the excitement of Sage's touch. Except this time the excitement of making love to Sage surged stronger than her own need. The thought of Sage's body responding, of hearing her breathless cries, and giving to her such exquisite joy thrilled her.

Quickened with desire, Deanne pressed her tongue deeper into Sage's mouth. With her hands, she touched the smooth skin reverently, caressed slowly over the tight shoulders, to cover the small perfect breasts, supple under loving fingers. She lingered over them, enjoying their softness and the feel of the stiffened nipples pressing into her palms. She wanted to surround them with her mouth and taste their tenderness with her tongue. She moved her lips with intent over the hollows of Sage's throat, down between her breasts. Slow caresses began their descent, traveling the length of her lover's body. Sage closed her eyes in apparent pleasure but remained reticent, her body still and unyielding.

Deanne's hand brushed lightly over the dark patch of hair. Her tongue teased a circle around a raised nipple. Before she could take it into her mouth, Sage grasped her head with both hands and shifted onto her side. She brought their lips together again, firmly, passionately. Excitement shot wildly through Deanne, blending with an undeniable yearning to bring her lover to orgasm. With anticipation at its peak, she slid ardently into the heat between Sage's legs. But almost immediately, before she could savor the warm wetness, Sage removed her hand and pulled Deanne into a tight embrace.

Stroking lovingly through Sage's hair, Deanne whispered, "Tell me what you need."

"It's not important," she answered softly. "As long as I can please you." Long fingers stroked tenderly over Deanne's cheek.

"It is important, honey. Please tell me."

Sage slipped from her arms. "I'll get us something to drink."

Deanne took her hand, left the bed, and stepped into Sage's arms. Her eyes questioned silently.

"It's a number of things, all tangled up together. The time's never been right to untangle it."

"We'll do it together."

"How patient are you?"

"I don't know," she whispered, applying little kisses to Sage's neck, and ear, and cheek. "Why don't you just kiss me?"

Passion took only a moment, took only the touch of their tongues, only the pressing of their breasts, only the placement of their hips against each another, to prove its power over them. A moan of desire escaped Deanne's throat and blended immediately with Sage's low sound of love. It was a power they enjoyed with their bodies, heated so quickly; succumbed to with both mind and emotion.

Their kisses deepened, becoming frantic in their need for each other, sending sensations racing wildly to the center of rhythmically moving hips. Short excited gasps accompanied Deanne's hands as they grasped Sage's buttocks. She tilted her pelvis and pressed herself into the wetness of her lover. Her body began to tremble. Deanne gasped, "I'm so close." Sage's hand slid over the tensing muscle of her buttock and into the wet heat. "Ohh . . . yes . . . Sage." She moved into the strokes, enjoying them for as long as she dared, then slid her body downward, out of Sage's reach. Her mouth swiftly followed the moist path between Sage's breasts and into the heat of her abdomen. Her hands caressed down the long back.

"Deanne," was all she said in a voice low and raspy.

Deanne's hands continued, caressing the lines of Sage's legs, long and beautiful, powerful where they met the round fleshy muscles of her buttocks. She held them in her hands, nuzzled her mouth carefully in the dark hair. Sage's fingers slid into Deanne's hair. They remained there, unmoving, offering no encouragement for Deanne to continue. Yet, despite the tensing of her body into a sudden shiver, they offered no resistance.

Cautiously, Deanne kissed the baby-smooth skin at the top of the long legs, not knowing if each second was one toward surrender, or one closer to Sage's mind overriding her body. She wanted to ready her quickly for the touch of her tongue, without tripping the wrong button. Deanne felt Sage's fingers move through hair and felt the tension filling her hands from muscles tilting Sage's pelvis forward. Deanne welcomed her with gentle movements of her mouth. With her hands she guided Sage's hips into their rhythm. Her senses were filled with the intoxicating scent of her, reeling in the thrill of her need. The sounds of desire, different from her own, surrounded and excited her. She wanted desperately to be inside her lover, to feel the tremor of her orgasm.

The defining line had disappeared for Sage. The definition between the pleasure she felt in satisfying a lover and what she felt now had become fuzzy. Nothing was ever too much to ask to fulfill her lover's desire; now she was aching selfishly for her own satisfaction. She widened her stance, giving access to a need long unfulfilled by a lover. Her fingers tightened into Deanne's hair. A long soft moan accompanied the first touch of Deanne's tongue. Her hips, in acquiescence, pressed forward into Deanne's full exploration. Her breathing stopped in expectation, as swirling touches repeatedly found their way back to the center of exquisite pleasure.

Sage's hips, now in fluid motion, became the measure for Deanne that told the urgency of the yearning. She pressed her mouth fully into rich velvety warmth and moved with teasingly different pressures. She listened to Sage's breathing shorten into raspy gasps. Hands left her hair to grasp her upper arms firmly, and the motion of her hips changed abruptly into a strong press. Hamstrings tightened under Deanne's hands and trembled with increased tension. The time was now. With stroke after perfect stroke, Deanne took Sage took her quickly, then entered her deep and full with her tongue. Sage's head dropped back in complete surrender. Her sinewy body arched in sublime rapture. She was held there in suspended ecstasy with the sound she raised to the ceiling bearing witness to her orgasm. Cries of joy found their freedom, echoing toward the ceiling. Her hips thrust forth once, then a second time, before she began to soften in Deanne's hands.

Wet kisses ascended the sensitive body, and Sage relaxed into Deanne's embrace. Her mouth went gently to Deanne's, tasting the fruit of her need. She felt sensitive and safe in this woman's arms. In a breathy voice still finding itself, she said, "It was wonderful. You were wonderful."

"Come and lie in my arms."

Deanne held Sage under warm down, stroking her head. "Have I told you yet," whispered Deanne, "that I love you?"

"With enviable skill." She raised her head from Deanne's chest. "No one's ever . . . I've never felt like this before."

"You trusted me enough to give up control?"

"Yes."

"It can be scary, with all the emotion that goes with it." Affectionately, she caressed Sage's head. "But the reward, sweet lover, is like no other."

"And I haven't forgotten yours," she said, cupping her hand over the still warm wetness. With a kiss deep and long, she entered. And with long slow strokes, she brought Deanne quickly to orgasm. She remained, blessedly tender, until Deanne lay in quiet lassitude in her arms. They stroked each other with featherlike touches of their fingertips.

"You know, you've spoiled me for any other woman," Deanne teased softly.

"Then, I'll have to keep you." She snugged her arms around her, and nuzzled kisses into her hair. Deanne looked up into thoughtful eyes, now fixed on the ceiling. "I remember NaNan telling me, more than once, 'I'm not worried about who you love, only that you can love, and love well.' I knew she meant acceptance of my sexuality. I did not know what love she spoke of until now. I never even knew pain, not even from this," she covered the scar with her hand. "Not from my father. Not until you walked away from me. Now I know, this is the love she meant, the kind that still brought tears to her eyes after forty years."

Lovingly, Deanne lightly touched Sage's face, tracing little turns of hair just over her ear and down the proud neck muscle. "Is that why you called me the keeper of your soul?"

Sage nodded. "And because I believe you feel the same kind of love."

"I do. That's why it terrified me so. Remember at the Longhouse when you asked me if I believed in omens? At the time I really didn't know, but ever since I met you, I've had fragments of visions and feelings that keep floating through my mind. They usually happened when I was around you. They were like strange feelings of déjà vu. I could never identify them or hold them long enough to know where they came from." Deanne rose from their embrace, and went to her overnight bag. She returned with the yellow handwritten page and clicked on the light beside the bed. "I have something I want you to read."

"I finally have you in my bed, and naked." She lightly caressed over Deanne's breast. "You have to know, reading is not high on my list."

Deanne snuggled back into Sage's arms with a smile. "I'll be right here all night, and all day tomorrow. I promise you, you won't miss five minutes of reading time. Besides, you're going to find this very interesting. I wrote it when I was in college. It's an account of a recurring dream from twenty years ago. I had it again the night before last." She watched intently and waited for Sage's reaction.

Sage read the account quickly, then her eyes went back to

the center of the page, where she read again. Even the stoic Sage couldn't keep her brow from furrowing as she checked the date at the top of the page. Suddenly, the lines on her forehead smoothed and disappeared. She looked up in astonishment. "It's NaNan's warrior, described exactly as she told me."

Deanne turned the paper over, pointing to the drawing of the warrior's marking. Then she gently traced the scar with her fingertips. "It's you."

Sage's eyes widened with amazement. She stared searchingly into Deanne's eyes, then once again at the words, as if to gain some other explanation. "I thought I understood." She leaned back against the headboard and shook her head slowly. "I never truly did."

"I hope this is something you can explain to me."

"I'll try, but I'm sure it's going to sound even more bizarre." Deanne waited patiently. "It was *orenda*."

"What, my darling, is *orenda*?"

Sage pulled the edge of the comforter around Deanne's shoulders and settled against the pillows. "My grandmother believed that each of us is filled with a spirit — a force, when respected, that connects us to each other, to our creator, and the world around us. Many Seneca, over the years, lost the will to nurture their spirit; they lost their belief in *orenda*. They can no longer hear or feel it. NaNan always feared such a loss; I think because she left her people to marry. She concentrated extremely hard on staying spiritually healthy."

Deanne kissed Sage on the cheek, and settled back next to her. "Now don't get distracted," she said to the smile on Sage's face. "I still don't know whether I'm confused or astounded. I certainly don't understand what *orenda* was doing in my dreams."

"Making me eternally grateful. You must have been very receptive; maybe you were searching and open to new direction in your life. I don't know. I don't pretend to have my grandmother's insights. I only know we are supposed to be most receptive to the voice of our spirit while we are sleeping. The dreams are messages, meant to help guide us in our lives. My own nights were too filled with nightmares to hear anything else. But NaNan was always analyzing and trying to understand their meaning. She thought I was blessed with a strong spirit, but, now I know how powerful *orenda* was in her."

"Strong enough to send her dreams all the way to me. If I hadn't experienced those dreams myself, I doubt if I could believe any of this possible."

Sage pointed to the date at the top of the paper. "I was eleven." She looked up and Deanne nodded. "The same year as my first successful vision quest. Many times before, I had visualized NaNan's warrior, concentrating on her somehow eased my emotional pain. But, that time, when I was eleven, I became one with her. And when I did, even the physical pain was gone. I'll explain," she said to the puzzled look she received. "To a young Indian, a vision quest is sort of a rite of passage where they go away alone, to visualize where their spirit draws strength. If they have nurtured their spirit well, they will be successful. For most, it was an animal, like the eagle, or the fox. For me, I always thought it was the warrior."

"And you were right."

"Much more so than I knew then. I had been beaten severely that day. NaNan came and took me with her. It was there, my face pressed against the soil of her garden, that it happened, that I first felt the strength of the warrior filling me, healing my broken body, soothing my bruised soul. All at once, my body was still. I was filled with a calmness that I had never felt. There was no anger, no fear, no pain. Being so young, I thought it meant that I'd be with NaNan from then on and no longer have to endure pain. I was only partially right."

"I wonder if NaNan knew her dreams were about you, if she ever sensed that they were received."

The dark eyes were distant now, reflective. "I asked her

once . . . I must have been about seventeen . . . if she had dreamed lately of the warrior, and she said, 'I haven't seen her for a while. But I don't worry. She is strong, and safe now.' "

Deanne's response was a soft whisper. "My god, she knew."

Sage nodded. "She knew she had done everything a caretaker, and a shaman, could do for me."

"She passed the responsibility on, made me the caretaker."

"Of my heart, and my body . . . as I am of yours." She smoothed her fingers gently over Deanne's uplifted face. "I'm not sure who intrigues me more, that beautiful, mystical old woman or you."

Deanne cuddled in tightly against her lover.

"Cold?"

"Mmm, no. You know I'm going to meet her some day."

"Well . . ." Sage wrapped her snugly in her arms. "I plan to be there when you do." She kissed her sweetly on the lips. "Would a house with a southern view, opening onto a deck and overlooking a quiet lake shore, be a good place for an author?"

"It will be a perfect place for an author."

About the Author

Marianne Martin currently resides in Michigan and is a writer and a professional photographer. After many years of teaching in the public school system, she first turned her hobbies into a career as a photojournalist with the *Michigan Women's Times*. An athlete since childhood, she has been a successful basketball and softball coach at the high school and amateur levels and a field hockey coach at the collegiate level. All of her not-so-leisure time in recent years has been spent working with her father to design and build her own home. The experience, wrapped around bruises, splinters, and a powerful sense of achievement, has taught her more about herself than she ever would have guessed.

She is the author of the following best-selling novels: *Mirrors* and *Love in the Balance,* published by Bella Books, *Dawn of the Dance,* and *Never Ending,* the sequel to *Legacy of Love.*

Her short stories can be found in three anthologies published by Naiad Press: *Lady Be Good, The Touch of Your Hand,* and *The Very Thought of You.*

Publications from
BELLA BOOKS, INC.
the best in contemporary lesbian fiction

P.O. Box 201007   Ferndale, MI 48220
Phone: 800-729-4992
www.bellabooks.com

LOVE IN THE BALANCE by Marianne K. Martin. 256 pp.
The classic lesbian love story, back in print!
ISBN 1-931513-08-2 $12.95

THE COMFORT OF STRANGERS by Peggy J. Herring.
272 pp. Lela's work was her passion . . . until now.
ISBN 1-931513-09-0 $12.95

CHICKEN by Paula Martinac. 208 pp. Lynn finds that the
only thing harder than being in a lesbian relationship is
ending one.   ISBN 1-931513-07-4 $11.95

TAMARACK CREEK by Jackie Calhoun. 208 pp. An intriguing story of love and danger.   ISBN 1-931513-06-6 $11.95

DEATH BY THE RIVERSIDE: 1st Micky Knight Mystery by
J.M. Redmann. 320 pp. Finally back in print, the book that
launched the Lambda Literary Award winning Micky Knight
mystery series.   ISBN 1-931513-05-8 $11.95

EIGHTH DAY: A Cassidy James Mystery by Kate Calloway.
272 pp. In the eighth installment of the Cassidy James
mystery series, Cassidy goes undercover at a camp for
troubled teens.   ISBN 1-931513-04-X $11.95

MIRRORS by Marianne K. Martin. 208 pp. Jean Carson and
Shayna Bradley fight for a future together.
ISBN 1-931513-02-3 $11.95

THE ULTIMATE EXIT STRATEGY: A Virginia Kelly
Mystery by Nikki Baker. 240 pp. The long-awaited return of
the wickedly observant Virginia Kelly.   ISBN 1-931513-03-1 $11.95

FOREVER AND THE NIGHT by Laura DeHart Young.
224 pp. Desire and passion ignite the frozen Arctic in this
exciting sequel to the classic romantic adventure *Love on
the Line*.   ISBN 0-931513-00-7 $11.95

WINGED ISIS by Jean Stewart. 240 pp. The long-awaited
sequel to *Warriors of Isis* and the fourth in the exciting
Isis series.   ISBN 1-931513-01-5 $11.95

ROOM FOR LOVE by Frankie J. Jones. 192 pp. Jo and
Beth must overcome the past in order to have a future
together.   ISBN 0-9677753-9-6 $11.95

THE QUESTION OF SABOTAGE by Bonnie J. Morris.
144 pp. A charming, sexy tale of romance, intrigue, and
coming of age.   ISBN 0-9677753-8-8 $11.95

SLEIGHT OF HAND by Karin Kallmaker writing as
Laura Adams. 256 pp. A journey of passion, heartbreak
and triumph that reunites two women for a final chance
at their destiny.   ISBN 0-9677753-7-X $11.95

MOVING TARGETS: A Helen Black Mystery by Pat Welch.
240 pp. Helen must decide if getting to the bottom of a
mystery is worth hitting bottom.   ISBN 0-9677753-6-1 $11.95

CALM BEFORE THE STORM by Peggy J. Herring. 208
pp. Colonel Robicheaux retires from the military and
comes out of the closet.   ISBN 0-9677753-1-0 $12.95

OFF SEASON by Jackie Calhoun. 208 pp. Pam threatens
Jenny and Rita's fledgling relationship.   ISBN 0-9677753-0-2 $11.95

WHEN EVIL CHANGES FACE: A Motor City Thriller
by Therese Szymanski. 240 pp. Brett Higgins is back in
another heart-pounding thriller.   ISBN 0-9677753-3-7 $11.95

BOLD COAST LOVE by Diana Tremain Braund. 208 pp.
Jackie Claymont fights for her reputation and the right to
love the woman she chooses.   ISBN 0-9677753-2-9 $11.95

THE WILD ONE by Lyn Denison. 176 pp. Rachel never
expected that Quinn's wild yearnings would change her
life forever.   ISBN 0-9677753-4-5 $12.95

SWEET FIRE by Saxon Bennett. 224 pp. Welcome to
Heroy — the town with the most lesbians per capita than
any other place on the planet!   ISBN 0-9677753-5-3 $11.95

**Visit
Bella Books
at
www.bellabooks.com**